Counting on Christmas

Counting on Christmas

Ken White

White & Wilkinson

Counting on Christmas

Author photo by James A. Ewing.
Silver Bell by Ron Wilkinson.
All other photos by Ken White.

Published in the United States of America
ISBN: 978-1-7340222-3-0 (Soft Cover)
ISBN: 978-1-7340222-5-4 (Case Bound)
ISBN: 978-1-7340222-6-1 (Cloth Bound)
ISBN: 978-1-7340222-7-8 (eBook)
1. Fiction / General
2. Fiction / Holiday
3. Fiction / Family

Library of Congress Control Number: 2020906853

Summary: Heartbroken when a precious holiday keepsake is stolen and her Christmas-themed business is threatened, a young woman who believes Christmas is the key to happiness learns life-changing lessons about love, family, community, and the true meaning of Christmas when she is visited by the ghosts of loved ones on Christmas Eve.

2430 Tully Road, Suite 20-058 | Modesto, California
95350 USA 1.209.567.0600 |
http://www.whitewilkinsonpub.com/

Dedication

To Madre and Daddy-O, who taught their children that giving was more important than receiving. Although we loved everything they gave us.

Special Thanks

Robin. My family. Carl Baggese. Ron Wilkinson. Bob Barzan. Barb Doyon. Jim Cirile. And to the creators of Christmas memories past, present, and yet to come.

Chapter 1

"Forever is composed of nows."
– Emily Dickinson, American Poet

It's a crisp autumn day in the Central Valley. The sun burns bright in the lapis blue skies above Modesto, California. Fiery fall colors etch the sky. The cool air smells of maple and woodsmoke. Soft seasonal music plays in the distance. The courthouse clock chimes the noon hour.

No matter what was happening in my life, I could always count on Christmas to make me happy.

Downtown Modesto is decorated with traditional Thanksgiving symbols and Day of the Dead (*Dia de los Muertos*) imagery. Wooden pilgrims and ceramic turkeys, candy skulls and brightly embroidered skirts and shirts fill the storefronts. People walk the streets, window shopping and greeting other shoppers. For a big town, Modesto is a small town at heart. Everyone knows everyone and everything.

The faint seasonal music transforms into a choir singing a traditional Christmas carol.

In my home town, we like getting a jump on Christmas.

The Bedford Falls Shop is located in one of the

original buildings constructed along Tenth Street. Once upon a time, Tenth Street was known for cruising: teenagers driving their cars up and down looking for some fun. It was an uncomplicated, more innocent time.

Inside the front display window of the shop sits a miniature, snow-covered village with replicas of the various locations from the movie It's a Wonderful Life. Fluffy cotton fabric blankets the village in simulated snow. Dangling on a string of red ribbon is a tiny silver bell ornament. It tinkles.

Outside of town, a few miles from the decorated storefronts and busy shoppers, the Tuolumne River snakes through a hibernating Legion Park. It's the week before Thanksgiving. The need is great. The line of homeless is long. Beneath a park shelter, tables are piled high with turkey dinner and all the trimmings. Men, women, and children file past the volunteers, who smile, as they ladle out the food, adding an encouraging word or two.

Jessica Rivers places a fresh dinner roll on each plate. At thirty, she's a bit of a hippie chick; a throwback to the sixties. Her bright evergreen eyes twinkle. An elfin Stevie Nicks, she wears a short Santa suitcoat with leggings, one red and one green. Her hair is also streaked red and green. One intricately braided strand of hair, tied with a bough of holly, cascades down her back.

"Happy Thanksgiving," she cheerfully says to a young homeless mother holding an infant girl. The woman takes the offering. Averting her eyes, she walks away.

A painful memory washes across Jessica's face, as she watches the mother and child disappear into the crowd.

"There's so many of them, Melissa," she says. "And so young."

"It's heart-breaking," replies Melissa Rivers, who stands next to her younger sister, handing out packets of butter. Melissa is four years older than her sibling.

"We're so lucky," Jessica continues.

"There but for fortune go you or me," Melissa answers.

"I count my blessings every day."

"Instead of sheep."

"Instead of reindeer."

They both chuckle.

"I'm glad we'll all be together this year, Jess."

"*If the fates allow*," Jessica sings the line from the Christmas song, "Have Yourself a Merry Little Christmas." She has a beautiful voice.

Jessica first heard that song when Judy Garland sang it in the movie, *Meet Me in St. Louis*. Garland and film director Vincente Minelli, who Garland would later marry, had asked Hugh Martin, the lyricist, to change the lyrics to make them more upbeat, which he did, changing the lines "It may be your last / Next year we may all be living in the past" to "Let your heart be light / Next year all our troubles will be out of sight." Another change he made for the film's producers was altering "Through the years, we all will be together if the Lord allows" to "if the fates allow" to remove any religious connotation, which might hurt ticket sales. The song became popular with troops overseas during World War II. Martin would make more changes for another great singer. Frank Sinatra asked the songwriter to "jolly" up one of the lines for his Christmas album, *A Jolly Christmas*. He revised the line "Until then we'll have to muddle through somehow" to "Hang a shining star upon the highest bough." It was, and remains, a classic Christmas song.

An older woman stops in front of Jessica. She has white hair, cracked spectacles, and wears a threadbare red skirt and a very tattered, very ugly sweater with an embroidered Santa Claus. A battered flute hangs from her black leather belt.

"Nothing ever happens by chance," she says, eyeing Jessica.

"It's a song I enjoy. That's all. About being together at Christmas."

"You can't always get what you want, you know."

"I'm grateful for what I have."

"You can't save everyone."

"I do what I can when I can. "

"You've got to take care of yourself."

"I do the best I can."

"You can't please everyone. You need to please yourself."

"I've been told that before."

The woman looks her up and down.

"Why do you dress like some old hippie?" she asks.

"I like the way it makes me feel."

"The sixties are dead."

"It was a better time. People helped people. People changed things."

"You can't live in the past."

"I don't want to live in the past. I just don't want to lose it."

"You can't control a river."

"I can try."

"Be careful. If you don't know where you're going, you might not get there."

The woman places the flute to her lips. She plays a haunting song as she moves off.

The food is gone. The tables are packed. The volunteers have left for home and family. The homeless have moved on in search of safe shelter.

Jessica kicks the dirt lining the bank of the Tuolumne River. Melissa kneels beside her. She takes photos with an expensive digital camera. Jessica stares at the water flowing directly in front of her. She looks upstream at where the water comes from. Her gaze then sweeps downstream to where the water goes.

"Everything is connected," she muses.

"What's that?"

"The past flows into the present and feeds the future," Jessica answers.

"Everything changes and nothing stands still. Everything flows and nothing abides."

"Except the Dude," Jessica says with a smile.

Chapter 2

The College Neighborhood is a tidy, established community of California ranch-style homes.

Brightly lit *luminarias* line the brick walkway leading to the front door of Jessica's festively decorated home. In imitation of the same traditional holiday lighting in Santa Fe, these paper bags are weighted down with sand and illuminated from within by a candle. The *luminarias*, or *farolitos*, as some in New Mexico prefer to call them, are intended to light the way to the stable for Mary and Joseph.

Inside the Southwest-style home, the halls are decked out for Christmas.

In the kitchen, the countertop is empty of electrical appliances. The juicer is manual. Coffee is made on the stovetop using a French press. Flour is ground from wheat. Bread is toasted in the fireplace.

In the master bedroom, an old dial radio provides low-tech tunes and time-telling. Made by RCA Victor, it has mechanical hands instead of a digital display.

In the window nook of the dining room, a rotating color wheel casts light on a well-used "Alcoa" aluminum tree, circa 1960, handed down from Jessica's mother, Cora. It's seen better days. Scotch tape holds some of the aluminum "needles" in place on each of the metal rod limbs stuck into a wooden tree trunk pole.

In the sun porch, an old music box plays "Frosty the Snowman," as a tiny plastic Santa skates in circles on a mirrored pond. Purchased from the Sears, Roebuck & Company mail order catalog, it, too, was handed down and is a bit tired looking. A circle has been etched into the reflective surface of the mirror pond where Santa has skated over the years. Each season, Jessica winds the music box, sets Santa at a spot on the circle, and waits to see him jerked into place, as a rotating magnet below the surface circles by.

In the living room, a collection of hand-made nativities from around the world is arrayed on an antique cedar chest. Purchased during her many travels, one set is made of soapstone, another of tin, yet another of clay, and one of wood, arrayed in front of the aged plastic figurines and wooden manger of the original nativity that sat in her childhood home's family room.

Each piece of living room furniture is a refurbished family heirloom, with most of the reconditioning having been done by Jessica. There is an easy chair reupholstered in red and gold fabric with an oriental symbol on the cushion, a wooden coffee table cut down from a dining room table, and a set of chairs and couch inherited from her mother. The couch cradles stuffed Christmas animals and characters, including the scruffy monkey she was given as a child when she had her tonsils removed.

Draped across the couch is a woven cloth throw featuring an image of the main street of Bedford Falls, an item which she carries in her store. The throw and the collection of replica buildings in her store's display window were the first of the many collectibles that inspired her to open the shop.

Stacked on coffee and side tables, shelves, and the floor are books about Christmas. Nothing but Christmas. Fiction, non-fiction, poetry, children's, and cookbooks. *A Christmas Carol*, *The Aussie 12 Days of Christmas*, *'Twas the Night Before Christmas*, *Hiddensea*, *The Nutcracker*, *Help! Christmas is Coming and I'm Not Ready*, *Madeline's Christmas*, *Everything I Need to Know About Christmas I Learned From a Little Golden Book*, Christmas songbooks, and some Debbie Macomber novels.

Other flat surfaces are covered with various holiday knick-knacks, candles, musical matchboxes, and a lighted ceramic Christmas tree; children's building blocks that spell Merry Christmas; framed photographs from past Christmases; a Russian nesting doll purchased and painted in a Christmas theme during her trip to St. Petersburg; various scented candles; a glass enclosed, blown glass ornament of the McHenry Mansion; Christmas cards sent from Taiwan by a high school friend; and a stuffed Mickey Mouse, Grinch, and snowman.

Hanging from the fireplace mantle is a beautifully embroidered stocking with a southwest design, featuring an ornamented saguaro cactus and howling coyote, done by her father, Daniel Rivers, Sr., and mother. Beside it is a row of vintage Christmas stockings, including Jessica's first stocking. Red and white with a stenciled image of Santa, his sleigh, and reindeer, her name is written at the top in ink in her mother's careful handwriting. Because there were five children, her mother wanted to make sure there were no mistakes or hurt feelings.

A piano is covered with colorful Santa Claus figures, inherited, purchased, or gifted over the years. Her most treasured are the ones made of ceramic, wood, and flowing fabric. There is also a wooden Santa with a wind-up music box and a jolly ceramic one, as well as a home-made St. Nick with the face of musician Slim Whitman stuck on a Santa body and crowned with a Santa cap. Slim, or "Slime," as some of Jessica's friends call him, was a country music singer, who had been one of the first to sell his albums on television. That's when Jessica's mom and dad fell in love with him.

A 10-foot-tall, live Christmas tree towers in the floor-to-ceiling window of the living room. It's covered in old-school ornaments. It's strung with '50s-era colored lights. And topped with a star. A beautiful tree skirt created by Jessica's mom and dad, with embroidered Christmas images, encircles the base of the tree. Unfortunately, it had been scorched in spots by the tree lights, which burned hotter than modern lights. She had kept it anyway, as a reminder now that they were both gone.

A long-playing record spinning round on a classic turntable plays Dean Martin singing, "Let It Snow." Jessica preferred the sound of vinyl, which is why she kept her Pioneer turntable, McIntosh tuner and amplifier powering Sony floor speakers. The sound seemed warmer and truer.

Jessica adjusts an ornament on one of the upper branches of the green tree. Staring at the lights, she squints her eyes. She smiles at a memory. Each year, since she had seen her first Christmas tree, once the lights were strung on the tree, she would lie on her back, peer up through the branches, and scrunch her eyes so the colored lights blurred. It was relaxing and resembled lights seen through fog or rain.

She wears a sweatshirt embroidered with a Sprint race car and the words, "Merry Christmas."

Her father had loved car races. He would have raced if he hadn't met her mom and had kids. Because he couldn't realize that youthful dream, he went to as many races as he could. Stock cars, Sprint cars, open-wheel cars. He had caught a NASCAR race at Sears Point once, but had never made it to Indianapolis, another dream unrealized. His heroes were drivers named Foyt, Unser, and Jones. Each year, he would listen to the Indy 500 on the radio and write down where each car was at each lap. He had embroidered this sweatshirt and wore it at the last Christmas before he passed away from an aortic aneurysm. The aneurysm was the result of a car wreck that happened coming home from the Stockton 99 Speedway late on a Saturday one summer.

"I hate Christmas," a male voice says from near the tree.

"It's never as bad as you think," Jessica replies.

"Sure, it is."

"You don't have to believe everything you think."

Michael Rivers, the forty-year-old big brother, toys with an ornament stenciled with a snow scene. He holds a Bloody Mary in the other hand.

"Careful. That's for the store," Jessica cautions, as she gently removes the ornament from his hand.

"Dad did that," Michael says, pointing at her sweatshirt.

"He did. And taught me."

"I don't get the boys this Christmas. She does. I get Thanksgiving."

"Be thankful you get that."

"It's tough on them. It's confusing. They don't know who to please. I think they're starting to hate it as much as I do."

"They're children, Michael. They'll figure it out."

"I should skip Christmas."

"Bah, humbug!"

"I'm not Scrooge, Jessica."

"Sure, you are."

"Didn't use to be."

"No, you loved Christmas. Almost as much as me."

"Life will do that."

"There was a time you couldn't wait for Christmas."

"I miss those days. I miss the old neighborhood. It was better when we were kids."

"Everything was."

"Not everything. Less complicated, maybe," he adds.

"Experiencing Christmas as a child. That's magical. Just pure, innocent joy."

"I could use a cup of that spirit right now."

"Christmas is about being a kid again. It's about giving gifts. Sharing. It's about being out of school. Remember what that first day of Christmas break was like?"

"Freedom. No homework. 'No more teacher's dirty looks.'"

"Christmas is about sugar canes. It's about feeling good. It's about no obligations. It's about cookies and eggnog. It's about believing. It's about Peace on Earth. It's about optimism. And hope."

"Wow, what wound you up?"

Jessica holds up her mug.

"Pumpkin latte," she answers.

"I need to get me some of that."

"You know, Michael, we were lucky. We had parents who loved us and each other. Who loved Christmas. And family. Who would do anything to make us happy."

"And spent time with us. It was easier being a child then."

"You could learn from them."

"Learn what?"

"You could spend more time with Taylor and Ethan and less time at the office."

"I want to leave them something when I'm gone. Something more than we got. In case something happens."

That catches Jessica off-guard. She's not sure she heard right. And, if she did, if he's serious about what he said. She changes the subject.

"How's Rachael?" she asks.

"Good."

"Is she helping you figure things out?"

"A little."

"The boys like her?"

"They do. It took some time."

"How's she feel about Christmas?"

"Bad as you."

"Better get with the program then."

"Won't be in the pre-nup. If there is one."

Jessica is surprised again, but in a more hopeful way.

"I wish it was winter and Christmas all year round," she says, then sings, "*Let it snow, let it snow, let it snow.*"

That enchanting voice again.

"'If I could work my will, every idiot who goes about with 'Merry Christmas' on his lips, should be boiled with his own pudding, and buried with a stake of holly through his heart!'"

Michael recites Scrooge's line from *A Christmas Carol* with a smile on his lips, but there's a kernel of truth beneath the grin.

"You keep Christmas in your way, dear brother, and I'll keep it in mine."

Michael shivers.

"I hate the cold," he says. "Give me summer. I'll take Honolulu over Jackson Hole."

"I wouldn't mind being there now. With all the schussing and the potsing."

He glances out the living room window at the gathering clouds then at the turntable surrounded by once state-of-the-art audio components.

"Whether it's the seasons or technology, change is a good thing," he says.

"There's too many things changing," Jessica replies. "I can't keep up with it. Besides, what has change ever done for me?"

"Change happens, Jess. Change happens. It wins every time. It's inevitable. Like – "

"I know. Like death and 'taxis'."

They both smile at her play on words.

Jessica moves to the couch. Piles of paper are neatly stacked on the coffee table in front of her. She cradles her mug of warm tea.

Michael sits at a nearby antique wooden card table. It's covered with a complex Christmas puzzle. He immediately fits a piece. He sets his wet glass on the table. Jessica slips a coaster beneath it.

"My Christmas list is done," Jessica says. "Secret Santa names are drawn. The Christmas cards are in the mail."

She hands him an envelope.

"Special delivery."

Michael opens the envelope and removes the card. It's hand-made with beautiful calligraphy.

"Saved a stamp," he comments. "You're learning. You'll make it big in spite of yourself."

A darkness flashes across Michael's face, as he recalls an uncomfortable memory. He opens the card. It reads: "To the best big brother in the world. I wouldn't be who I am without you. *Mele kalikimaka* (Merry Christmas)."

Jessica hands him a soft package simply wrapped in white tissue paper with red ribbon.

"I wanted you to have this for Christmas."

"Well, 'Happy Holidays' to me."

"You mean, 'Merry Christmas'."

"No, I mean 'Happy Holidays'."

"If that's what you believe."

"It covers a multitude of sins."

"As long as it makes you happy."

Michael opens the present. It's a white pullover with an embroidered red Nutcracker. Michael's face registers confusion and disappointment. This isn't his style.

"You shouldn't have."

And he means it. He sets the present aside.

It's not the reaction Jessica was hoping for. Ever the optimist and not willing to let him spoil her Christmas, she pushes on.

"If everyone is okay with it, I'd like to have the Rivers' family Christmas here this year."

"Let's keep it at my place. One more year. It'll feel less empty now that the boys won't be there."

"You sure?"

"I am."

"Have you thought any more about us making donations to worthy causes instead of doing the gift exchange?"

"Jess – "

"Not this year, next year."

Michael slips the Christmas card back inside the envelope.

"Take a breath, Jess. You can't orchestrate the future."

"You can't stop me."

"That's not the way the world works. I've been

around longer. I've seen it."

"Now you're just being the big brother. And a cynic."

"No, a realist. Just being practical."

Michael gets up and walks to the collection of nativities. He picks up the baby Jesus.

"You're rushing it a bit, aren't you?" he says.

"It's never too early for Christmas."

She follows. She gently takes the figure from him and puts it back. She returns to the couch.

"Studies say people who trim trees earlier are happier," she adds. "While people who decorate their houses sooner are friendlier."

"Likely underwritten by Walmart."

"It's true. You can look it up."

"What, you're embracing technology?"

"No, I meant the library."

"You're such a creature of habit."

"Christmas is comforting. It's something I can count on. Maybe the only thing."

"Doesn't it get old?"

"What?"

"Being stuck in Christmas. In the past."

"All our family, especially Mom, loved Christmas."

The phone rings. Michael glares at the old red Princess phone.

"I'll let the machine get it."

"It couldn't hurt to get an actual phone."

"It does the job."

"The past isn't what it used to be."

"Neither is the present."

Michael joins Jessica on the couch. He sifts through a basket of old photos on the coffee table.

"Christmas is a good time for looking back," Jessica says.

"Nostalgia is just bad memory. It was once considered a disease, you realize. A pathology."

"There's nothing wrong with me."

"It's lonely there, you know."

"I don't need anything. Or anybody."

"We all need somebody. To lean on."

"I can take care of myself."

"You're too damned independent."

"Stubborn, you mean."

"That, too."

"Tone of voice, Michael. It's condescending."

"If it fits …"

"'Sides, you have no room to talk."

"Can't imagine what you're referring to," he replies, grinning.

"The Mud Bowl. All you old guys reveling in past glories. Talk about sickness."

"It's one day, not 365."

"Except when you're planning it, texting or emailing about it, posting photos, organizing the banquet, Facebooking about it, printing up T-shirts – "

"Okay, okay. Point made."

"Don't forget the video. How many hours do you put in on that?"

"Speaking of which."

"Don't worry. I'm rehearsed and ready."

"The video wouldn't be the same without our song."

"Proud to prolong the juvenilia."

Michael reaches for his coat draped over the back of the couch. He removes a small, flat, holiday box with a tiny bow from the inside pocket. He hands it to her.

"A small token of appreciation for taking the time."

"I thought you hated Christmas."

"Just open it."

She does. Inside is a Christmas tree pin dotted with rubies and emeralds.

"It's beautiful, Michael. And expensive. I'm not sure I deserve it."

"You absolutely do."

He takes it and pins it to her Christmas sweatshirt.

She hugs her brother.

"I'm just saying," he continues. "It'd be nice if you had something – someone – permanent instead of dipping in and out of people's lives – our lives – like some kind of 'Christmas Gypsy'."

"I've got Brandon. For now."

Michael reacts, confused.

She ignores it.

"Josh was perfect for you."

"Doesn't do much good when he's gone."

Jessica focuses on her brother a moment, thinking how different he is from her old boyfriend, Josh, and how similar he is to her fiancé, Brandon.

"He was a nice guy," Michael says.

"He is."

"See you Saturday."

"Saturday, it is."

Michael collects his coat and takes another look at the Nutcracker pullover before tossing it across his arm and leaving.

Later that day, Jessica wanders through the kitchen, watering her collection of healthy, well-tended houseplants. She carefully cleans a blossoming Christmas cactus. She stops and looks out a set of corner windows.

The mirrored glass of the adjacent windows creates the illusion of Jessica with two faces, standing in two doorways. Like Janus contemplating the road behind and the road ahead. One face looking backward, one face looking forward.

A beam of sunlight highlights the reflection on her left – the past.

Chapter 3

The Bedford Falls Shop is a boutique store located on the ground floor of an original Kress "five and dime" Department Store. The building has been renovated, as much of the downtown has over the years – renovated or demolished.

Modesto is only now recovering from years of urban renewal that changed the heart and soul of the downtown. As the center of a growing agricultural region, it attracted people downtown to shop, work, and be entertained. Unfortunately, parking lots and empty lots seemed to often replace some of the historically significant structures that were torn down. As a result, many businesses fled to the outskirts of town. A few of the historic buildings were renovated, including the State Theatre, built in 1934. Over the years, new facilities were built to help resurrect the downtown, including city and county offices at Tenth Street Place and the Gallo Center for the Performing Arts. A handful of architecturally significant buildings have been saved from the wrecking ball, including the Stanislaus County Courthouse, a classic midcentury modern structure. The Beaty Building and the *El Viejo* Post Office are two more reminders of a bygone era, as is the McHenry

Mansion, an Italianate Victorian built in 1882. Other notable architectural jewels still standing include the Modesto Arch, the George Cressey residence, the Hawke residence, the Lion Bridge, and the first downtown home of J.C. Penney. Some noteworthy buildings of Central Valley Modernism include the former City Hall Building and County Courthouse, the Heckendorf house, and the Stanislaus County Hall of Records. Modesto even has its own typeface designed by typographer Jim Parkinson.

Jessica remembered the spirit of the old downtown and the many hours she had spent there while growing up. That's why she decided to locate her business in one of the buildings that needed rescuing. She only hoped she and the other tenants would prove prosperous enough to save the space.

The shop is filled with Christmas decorations and memorabilia. As the name suggests, most of the merchandise is related to the movie, *It's a Wonderful Life*. Ornaments, miniature buildings and figurines, blankets, cards, puzzles, snow globes, and calendars.

Jessica had been in love with the movie since the first Christmas she saw it. Due to a clerical error, the 1946 movie had accidentally gone into the public domain in 1974, which meant television stations could broadcast it royalty-free. In 1993, Republic Pictures, which still owned the rights to Philip Van Doren Stern's story, "The Greatest Gift," which the movie was based on, sued to enforce their copyright. In 1996, they negotiated an exclusive license with NBC to show the film. Since then, it had been shown every Christmas. There was something deeply appealing about a man doubting and then witnessing the impact of his life, especially when that character was played by Jimmy Stewart.

Many consider *It's a Wonderful Life* to be the great American Christmas story. It was notable for several reasons, but especially for being the first film Frank Capra and Jimmy Stewart did following their service in World War II. Capra was a director, producer, and writer who was the creative force behind some of the major award-winning films of the 1930s and 1940s, including *It Happened One Night, Mr. Smith Goes to Washington*, and *Meet John Doe*. At 44, Capra had received a commission as a major in the U.S. Army. It was Capra's job to head a section on morale, reporting directly to Chief of Staff George Marshall, with the mission of explaining to soldiers why they were fighting. As part of his duties, Capra directed and produced seven documentary films. Other notable film directors who also did war documentaries included John Ford, William Wyler, George Stevens, and John Huston. Jimmy Stewart was the first major American movie star to enlist. At 33, he first served as a private in the Air Corps and was later promoted to lieutenant in the 445th Bombardment Group, a B-24 Liberator unit based in England. He finished his service as a colonel, having received the Distinguished

Flying Cross and the French *Croix de Guerre*.

Director Capra's only choice for the character of George Bailey was Stewart, who would later credit Capra for resurrecting his career by offering him the role. For Mary, he considered Jean Arthur, who had starred opposite Stewart in *Mr. Smith Goes to Washington* and Olivia de Havilland, who had starred in *Gone with the Wind*, before casting Donna Reed. For Mr. Potter, he looked at Charles Bickford and Claude Rains, among many others, before choosing Lionel Barrymore. For Uncle Billy, he considered Barry Fitzgerald and Walter Brennan before going with Thomas Mitchell. For Bert the cop, he thought about Barton MacLane and Robert Mitchum, eventually selecting Ward Bond. It's impossible to imagine anybody else in these iconic roles.

The film was shot at RKO Picture's Studios in Culver City and their Encino Ranch. Capra constructed the longest set ever built for an American movie up to that time. The closing snowstorm scene was shot in ninety degree weather, while the swimming pool scene was shot in the gym at Beverly Hills High. The scene at Mary's house where George finally kisses her was killed by the censors as being too sexy. Capra kept it in anyway.

The film didn't do well at the box office, or with critics. It was nominated for an Academy Award in five categories, including Best Picture, Best Director, and Best Actor, but lost in four of the five categories to *The*

Best Years of Our Lives, another postwar film, directed by Capra's colleague and business partner, William Wyler. *It's a Wonderful Life* was awarded a Technical Achievement Award for the development of a new method of simulating falling snow. It is now considered one of the greatest films of all time and is listed at number 11 on the American Film Institute's 100 best American films.

The city of Seneca Falls, New York, which claims to be the inspiration for Bedford Falls, holds a festival honoring the film each year.

One corner of Jessica's store sells children's books. On a child-sized table sits three children's Christmas books written by Jessica: *That Happiness Thing: A Hometown Fable*, *The 12 Days of Central Valley Christmas*, and *'Twas the Night Before Christmas ... In Modesto*.

In another corner is a collection of framed and unframed Christmas watercolors also done by Jessica.

The silver bell ornament that was hanging in the front window now dangles inside a glass display case. A certificate of authenticity indicates that it is the actual prop used in the Frank Capra movie. The small bell, which decorated the Bailey family Christmas tree, tinkled at the end of the film to signal that George Bailey's guardian angel, Clarence, had received his wings for helping George realize he really did have a wonderful life. Clarence had told George earlier in the movie that a bell rings every time an angel gets its wings. Clarence had been sent to earth hoping he might finally earn his wings.

Shoppers browse the shelves, display cases, and artificial trees adorned with ornaments.

Melissa, dressed in a costume similar to that worn by the character Violet Bick in *It's a Wonderful Life*, assists a hip twenty-something female. Violet was the perky young girl who had been vying for George's affections with Mary Hatch since they were all children. He was working at Gower's Drugstore soda fountain and they were there to flirt. She grew into a beautiful woman.

Jessica, costumed as the character Mary Bailey when she was renovating the old Grantham Place in the same movie, rings up a sale on the ancient cash register, which closely resembles the one in Martini's bar. PayPal, Apple Pay, Square, and Zelle aren't welcome here.

A burly man in his thirties chats with Jessica.

"Thanks again for posting the flyers and sending out the cards about the toy drive," he says.

"Happy to help, Barry."

"And making all those phone calls. That took time."

"I enjoy talking to people."

"You really are our 'Town Crier'."

"That's what they call me."

"I think I can speak for most people when I say we appreciate everything you do for the community. You're a true MoTown 'Energizer Bunny'."

"If it makes my home town a better place to live, then it's the least I can do."

"The flyers and cards were beautifully done. You're very talented."

"I appreciate the smell and feel of the paper and the paint. That's probably why I read books. And advertise in the newspaper and on the radio."

"Staying old school."

"And proud of it."

"It probably would've cost less and taken less time if you'd emailed, texted, or posted to Facebook."

"I don't own a cell phone or computer."

Barry is mildly stunned.

"How do you get along?" he asks.

"Quite nicely. Fewer distractions."

"Good for you."

"It is. And good for everyone if they'd unplug once in a while."

"Well, I don't know what I'd do without my toys."

"Try it. You might enjoy it."

"We'll see. Well, Happy Holidays, Jessica."

"Merry Christmas."

As Barry leaves, Melissa joins her sister.

"Why do you do that?" she asks.

"What?"

"Correct people when they say, 'Happy Holidays' instead of 'Merry Christmas'?" Melissa clarifies.

"'Tis the season, isn't it? I mean 'Happy Holidays' is so generic."

"Actually, it's respectful. Not everyone is a Christian. Different people, different religions, have different celebrations. Jews, Muslims, Buddhists, pagans. Each may celebrate this time of year, but for different reasons," Melissa explains.

"Ah, the winter solstice."

"December 21st. A bleak midwinter's day," Melissa says.

"The shortest day and longest night of the year. "

"In the dark and cold, we seek warmth and solace in family and community. Feasts, festivals, and celebrations are held because it means the return of the sun. The return of hope," Melissa adds.

"Hope Solo that is."

"Or Bob Hope."

They both laugh.

A ten-year-old boy touches the display case holding the silver bell ornament.

"Beautiful isn't it," Jessica says.

"Is it magical?" he asks.

"I think so."

Behind the boy, a male voice asks, "Is it real?"

Jessica looks up. A tense young man in his twenties points at the ornament.

"Certificate says it is," Jessica answers.

"Where'd you get it?"

"A gift."

"Valuable?"

"To me."

"Good to know," he replies.

The shop door tinkles, as the young man exits the store.

Sniffing the air where he was, Melissa says, "That one needs a bath."

Jessica grimaces in agreement.

"I've been reading this book," Jessica says. "*The Christmas Box*. One of the characters asks, 'Which of the senses do you think is most affected by Christmas?' What's yours?"

Melissa points at her camera, which sits behind the sales counter.

"Sight, of course," she answers. "What about you?"

"All of them. For different reasons. The creamy eggnog, the soft tree boughs, the music box carols, the peppermint candles, and the colored lights."

"That's sensational," Melissa says, smiling at her clever wordplay.

"I can taste, touch, hear, smell, and see all the cheery things that make me happy this special time of the year," Jessica continues. "I wish the feeling could last all year long."

Chapter 4

The shop is closed. Jessica sits alone. She sips a peppermint tea and ponders the winter solstice. *Because it marks both the end and beginning of another solar year,* she recalls from some past class, *it's associated with transformation. With endings and beginnings, with death and rebirth. What will be her new direction?* she considers. *Perhaps to simply live life without thinking about the future.* She remembers something someone said: *"The path is the goal,"* which was a variation on Emerson's *"Life is a journey, not a destination."* To pursue something in the future is to always be searching. She thinks, *Perhaps living life well in the eternal now is something she can achieve and feel good about.*

Then she thought of Hope. Bob, not Solo. She loved Bob. He made her laugh. His *Road* pictures with Bing Crosby were ones she watched again and again. She especially appreciated his Christmas shows with the troops. Even though she was a pacifist and thought war was stupid, the result of too much testosterone and bruised male egos, she didn't blame the young men and women on the front lines. They were doing what they were asked by their country. She blamed the men who sent them there. Bob brought them a badly needed taste of home for the holidays. She loved him for doing that.

Jessica has many things to be thankful for this time of year, but she is especially thankful for the compassion and generosity of her community. Each year she is reminded of this when she participates in a number of pre-Thanksgiving events.

The first, following closely on the heels of Halloween, a holiday her youngest older brother Johnny loved, is a fundraiser the family started the year following his passing to honor his memory. When his wife, Kristi, died a few years later, also from cancer, the fundraiser celebrated them both. A local restaurant agreed to host the Sunday afternoon affair, which featured a silent auction and jam of local musicians who were family or friends. Anybody who had ever played with Johnny and Kristi was invited and nearly all sat in. Guys from his first and last bands, as well as most of the ones in-between, joined others to play songs Johnny had played or songs by musicians Johnny respected, including the Beatles, Neil Young, Cream, and Eric Clapton. One year, the family asked everyone to learn and play one of the songs from a CD Johnny completed weeks before he died. The interpretations of his songs were heartfelt and amazing. It was always a beautiful, if bittersweet, day that left the family, and Jessica in particular, pleasantly exhausted. Jessica was the one who kept the program moving and usually played with everyone. She particularly looked forward to playing with Dylan, the son of Allen George Mullens, Michael's best friend. Allen had died a couple years before Johnny. Dylan became a musician like his father. Instead of singing and playing flute, he played drums, likely inspired by all those times he saw his father, his father's friend Michael, and their mutual friends pounding rhythmically on ottomans and tables, vibrating drinks, silverware, and ashtrays over the edge. Johnny's artwork and his CD, as well as items donated by family and friends, were auctioned off. The money they raised helped fund Creation Station at the Gallo Center, an art and theatre summer camp, as well as scholarships for young artists and musicians, since Johnny was both a talented artist and musician. At the end of the day, everyone who attended realized how really good he had been.

The next function is "Home for the Holidays" at First United Methodist Church, which is Jessica's church and the church where she sings in the choir. It is basically a holiday bazaar, with an eclectic collection of home-made crafts and foods, as well as donated items like jewelry, clothes, books, and household items. There is always a breakfast brunch. Jessica volunteers each year. All funds help support the many community programs of the church, including various ministries, Heifer International, and Salvation Army Shelter Meals. The day could be mildly chaotic as people scrambled for one of a kind finds. Jessica always bought a couple jars of bread and butter pickle slices made by Edith Burchell. She also often found a vintage tablecloth or Christmas ornament. She loved being a part of, and supporting, her church community.

The First United Methodist Church had been a part of Modesto since 1871, with new churches being built by the congregation each time the existing church was outgrown. The newest building was finished in 1932 at Sixteenth and I Streets. It had been renovated a few times, mostly to make it earthquake safe. The sanctuary was airy, beautiful, and comforting. The Fellowship Hall had been the site of innumerable church and community, sacred and secular, occasions. Jessica and her family had grown up with many of the church families. Some of the parents, contemporaries of her folks, were still alive and active. Jessica and her sibs had participated in DeMolay and Job's Daughters, which were youth organizations for young men and women. Growing up, she rarely missed a Christmas Eve or Easter service. As an adult, she had joined the choir and become more involved with church activities. It was just one more way she could give back to the community that had given her so much.

Another gathering she rarely misses is the Stanislaus County Interfaith Council's Thanksgiving Celebration, which takes place each year on the Monday before Thanksgiving and is held at different churches and community venues. The evening features music, readings, and other expressions of gratitude from her home town's faith community. Buddhist, Christian, Hindu, Jewish, Muslim, Sikh, Unitarian Universalist, and other faith groups participate. Attendees are encouraged to bring canned goods and/or money to benefit Interfaith Ministries' Emergency Food Pantry and its goal of restoring dignity, health, and hope. Refreshments and fellowship follow the event. It is a memorable way to show respect and learn about the diversity of the community's faith traditions. Last year, Dylan had become an integral part of this event when he had gone to work for Interfaith in marketing and outreach.

Jessica pays it forward each year by participating in the Six Cups to College mentoring program. Offered through the Stanislaus County Office of Education, its goal is to improve access to college and increase the number of students completing an advanced degree. Interested students can enroll as early as their junior year of high school. Volunteer mentors are matched based on gender and career. Mentees and mentors meet in a public space like a coffee shop at least six times during the school year to have coffee and discuss the colleges they're interested in, the application process, financial aid, and other topics. In her first year, Jessica mentored a junior named Lauren at Modesto High School, who was interested in music. Last year, she mentored Kathleen at Thomas Downey High School, who was considering nursing. This year she is working with Connie, another

Downey student, who thought she might want to work in advertising. In a bit of serendipity, all three are cousins. Jessica is always pleasantly surprised by these talented and dedicated young women. She looks forward to seeing the impact they will have on their world.

Jessica also attempts each year to take a music class through Modesto Junior College's community education program. It's a way for her to continue her musical education and meet others inspired by music. In the past, she has taken classes in piano, ukulele, voice, guitar, and harmonica. This year, she is taking a beginning harp class, which emphasizes the Celtic harp. Her goal is to add another instrument to accompany her while performing during the holiday season.

The closet in Jessica's spare bedroom overflows with costumes inspired by her treasured Christmas films.

"I remember when you made this," Melissa says, holding a black velvet dress with a scalloped neckline and mermaid profile.

"*Love you didn't do right by me,*" Jessica sings, as Melissa waltzes around the room with the dress.

"You still wear it well," Melissa replies.

"It's hard not to look good."

"Rosemary had a little more padding than you."

"Just right for the era."

"I wonder what Bing would have looked like in this?"

"Bob would have been a better fit."

"I think you've made something for every one of our favorite movies."

"I'm still working on Olaf."

"And the pink bunny."

"I'm not sure I could wear that one."

"Ralphie had to."

"Poor boy."

Jessica flips through each costume, naming the flick which inspired it.

"*It's a Wonderful Life*, *White Christmas*, *The Bishop's Wife*, *Holiday Inn*, *A Christmas Story*, *Elf*."

"You've never done one for *The Nightmare Before Christmas*."

"That's a Halloween movie masquerading as a Christmas movie."

"Sally would be tough to recreate."

"Not as tough as *Jack Frost 2: Revenge of the Killer Mutant Snowman*."

"I can't even imagine that."

"Why would anybody make a horror Christmas movie?"

"There must be an audience."

"That explains why they were able to make other stinkers like *Santa with Muscles* or *Surviving Christmas* or *Silent Night, Deadly Night*."

"Is your song ready?"

"Ready as it ever will be."

"It'll be great. Always is."

Jessica holds up a small round mirror sort of shaped like a Grammy.

"I thank you for this award and your support. I couldn't have done it without you."

"Michael couldn't, either."

"It all evens out."

Chapter 5

Del Rio is located north of town. It's a wealthy neighborhood of large homes along the golf course occupied by members of the Del Rio Country Club. This is where Michael lives.

Judging from the outside of his house, it's impossible to tell it's coming on Christmas. There's a forlorn, solitary wreath on the front door. Inside, his house is ultra-modern. Spare. Lots of hard edges, stark colors, and stainless steel. A pre-lit, artificial tree squats forlornly undecorated in a corner of the family room. Child-like drawings of Santa and snowflake cutouts are magneted to the refrigerator, or taped to a window. It's a sharp contrast to Jessica's lived-in home.

One of the rooms serves as an office, editing suite, and recording studio. Signed sports memorabilia, industry award statues, and framed advertising agency and communication industry certificates fill the shelves and dot the walls.

Michael sits at a sound board connected to his Windows computer.

Jessica sits in a tiny, dimly lit sound booth, acoustic guitar cradled in her lap.

"I was beginning to panic," Michael says.

"That's what you do."

"It's my job."

"Have I ever let you down?" Jessica asks.

"Close a couple times."

"And what do they say about close?"

"It's only good in horseshoes – "

"And hand grenades."

Jessica plays a melody and sings a few lines.

"What's that?" he asks.

"A Christmas song I wrote. I'm working on it for the family gathering."

"What's it called?"

"'Child of Song'."

"It's good. You're good."

Jessica smiles, flattered, but slightly embarrassed.

"Of course, I tell you that every time I hear you," Michael adds.

"I never get tired of hearing it."

"At the ad agency, I work with a boatload of talented singers and songwriters. You're as good, or better, than most.

"That means a great deal coming from you."

"If you bought some pieces of gear, you could put some things out there. You could be another on-line phenom."

Jessica snickers.

"I'm serious."

"As only you can be," she replies.

"Deadly serious."

"I'm happy playing coffee shops and street corners."

"You're blowing it. You could be something. Be somebody. Unlike me."

That darkness crosses his face again.

"You gave it your best shot," Jessica says, noticing the look.

"It wasn't good enough. I wasn't good enough. You are."

"I'm fine the way I am."

Michael points at Jimmy Stewart captured in the movie poster for *It's a Wonderful Life*. A gift from Jessica, of course. She found it in a thrift store in West Hollywood. The store owner couldn't tell her if the person they bought it from had gotten it from Frank Capra's estate sale, or the archives of Liberty Films. Liberty Films was the production company founded by Capra and Samuel J. Briskin in April 1945. It produced two films. *It's a Wonderful Life* and the film version of the hit play, *State of the Union*.

"Don't be him. 'BC'."

"'BC'?"

"'Before Clarence.' He was a dreamer, not a doer. He didn't believe in himself. He didn't think he was worth anything or made a difference or had an impact. He thought he was a failure because he didn't achieve any of his dreams. He was foolish enough to think everyone – the world – would be better off without him."

"Now who's wound up?" Jessica asks.

Michael holds up his Mud Bowl coffee cup.

"Kahlúa-infused Columbian," he explains.

"That's not the way I saw George Bailey," Jessica replies.

"Of course not."

"He had everything he needed or wanted. Friends, family, community, and work he grew to love. Work that made a difference. He did good."

"Eventually, perhaps. It took some convincing. To finally see his own value. To recognize who he was, what he had to offer, and his role in life. It took a guardian angel. It took dying. To do good."

"Metaphorically."

"Don't let that happen to you."

"I'd like to be as successful and loved as he was."

"It was a fairy tale. There are no happy endings. No 'happily-ever-afters'."

"Let me have my delusions," she says.

"All I'm saying is you're better than you think."

"You're only saying that because you're my big bro."

"You are. You have more to offer than you can imagine."

"I'm okay with the way things are."

"For now."

Jessica moves closer to the microphone. She smiles,

but her eyes say something else.

"You know, I've been warned about not becoming you," she says.

"Wise advice. I'm tired of 'have to.' Tired of being responsible. The go-to guy. The one everyone counts on."

"We do count on you. Always have. You're the one who leads the way. That's always right."

"It's not easy being the first born, you know."

"I don't know, to be honest."

"Good and bad, you're the first to start the circle game. I was the experiment. Mom and Dad got to make all their mistakes on me."

"We thank you for that."

"They were tougher on me when it came to behavior, grades, and expectations. But, I was also their top priority, their one responsibility. It was worth it."

"By the time they got to me, it was pie."

A confused look from Michael.

"As in, 'easy as'."

He shrugs his shoulders.

"Over the years, I've done any number of stupid, selfish things to you guys," he says. "It wasn't right and I knew it. I didn't mean to do it. It simply seemed to happen. I felt badly about it, but couldn't seem to help myself."

"Sure, you could."

"I didn't often think things through. After I'd done

whatever I'd done, I'd invariably wish I could take it back. It was usually too late and the damage had been done."

"You weren't that bad."

"I wonder what it would have been like and how different the world would have been if I had been anywhere else in the birth order. But, that's not the way it played out."

"No, it wasn't."

"I was the care-taker. Then. Now. Always."

"I like where I am in the birth order."

"I wish I could say the same."

"You've got a wonderful life," she says and smiles, unable to let the opportunity to remind him slip by.

"That's what they say."

"You okay, Michael?"

"Enough therapy for the day. Let's get back to the task at hand. I need to get this done and edited. The Mud Bowl banquet waits for no one."

Contemplating her brother, Jessica recalls a particularly painful encounter with Michael shortly after he graduated from UC Davis and began applying to business schools.

"Merry Christmas," she said, as she handed him a monogrammed leather briefcase with a bright red bow stuck to it.

"This is nice. Very nice."

"I was going to get you an expensive fountain pen,

but I figure you needed something practical. Something you wouldn't need to write stories, compose songs, or draw things."

"Who told you?"

"Dan."

"I told him not to say anything."

"We can't keep secrets. We have Mom to thank for that."

"I was going to tell you."

"When?"

"As soon as I found out."

"Berkeley's MBA program will be lucky to have you."

"It was time to get serious. There's no future in writing."

"Not if you give up before you start."

"I have to make a living."

"You're a writer. A good writer."

"Not good enough."

"So now you're one of them."

"Who?"

"A suit. Not an artist."

"What do you want me to do?"

"Do what you were meant to do."

"Unfortunately, unlike you, I don't have that kind of freedom."

"Oh, the flakey little sister."

"That's not what I meant."

"Sure it is. I'm the Huck Finn of the family."

"I'm doing what I need to do. What I have to do."

He hadn't wavered. He'd graduated from Berkeley, got a job with Hal Riney's ad agency in San Francisco, soon went freelance, stayed in the Bay Area a few more years, and returned home to run his business remotely. He never looked back.

"Stand by."

Michael's voice disrupts the memory.

Jessica plays and sings a song about old friends, which she's rewritten to fit the unique elements of The Mud Bowl.

Chapter 6

Jessica walks past a downtown cash store. A table sits near the entrance. A salesman registers people for high interest rate credit cards.

Just beyond the table and down a side street, two men in their thirties exchange heated words. It's about to escalate.

Just then, a young mother cradling an infant passes by.

The salesman stops selling. The two men stop fighting.

Jessica and Melissa bask in the weak sunlight streaming through the windows of Jessica's sun porch. A VHS copy of the holiday movie, *The Gathering*, plays silently on the television.

Melissa flips through pages on her iPhone.

Jessica's eyes bore into her little sister.

"For once it would be nice to see your face and not the of your head," she says.

"You're no better," Melissa responds, pointing at the children's Christmas book lying open on Jessica's lap.

"You know me," Jessica answers. "Just an old-fashioned girl. I prefer analog over digital."

"Stuck in the past, you mean."

"Call it what you will. I don't have a problem being bored for more than a second."

"I'm not bored, believe me," Melissa says.

"Distracted then."

"It's important."

"Not as important as what you lose. "

"Like what?"

"Energy. Sleep. Patience. Health. And time. Especially time."

"As if there's enough hours in the day for you," Melissa accuses.

"To do the things I want to do. Things that make a difference. That make people smile."

"Just because you're doing good doesn't mean you're any less hassled, preoccupied, or busy as the rest of us."

"Time is relative to your state of motion. Technology speeds up time. When you're moving quickly with all these devices, time passes fast. Time literally flies."

"I don't have time to notice."

"Advertisers make promises and plugged-in people believe that technology improves our lives. Makes it more efficient."

"Advertisers have a loose affiliation with the truth. It's all subliminal seduction," Melissa answers.

"Technology keeps us from interacting in a meaningful way. It takes us away from the physical act of doing things."

"There are some physical acts I don't mind avoiding. Or embracing."

"Unplugging is similar to the back to the earth movement of the Sixties," Jessica continues. "People want to get back to a purer way of living. Back to the garden."

"Thank you, Joni."

"Back to a life in balance."

"I can dig it, *Koyaanisqatsi*."

"They want to rediscover hobbies, use their hands, get outdoors, interact with each other in a way that isn't dictated by bits and bytes," Jessica points out.

"I can juggle multiple tasks with both hands tied behind my back."

"Here's something you probably won't believe. The average person checks their phone 80 times a day."

"I need to Google that."

"That addiction is having serious effects on our health. From rewiring our brain to reducing our attention span to spiking our blood pressure and even making us more stupid," Jessica adds.

"That ain't true, gosh darn it."

"*New York Times* says it is."

"Liberal rag," Melissa answers, smiling and poking her sister in the ribs.

"Another thing. There's also the 'dumbing-down' of communication. Because people want a quick answer, we ask questions that get quick answers."

"It's efficient."

"It's lazy."

"What if I miss something?" Melissa asks.

"It can wait."

"What if it's important?"

"It's never that important."

"What if I'm lost in the middle of nowhere?"

"Assuming you have service."

"It could save my life."

"I'll give you that one," Jessica concedes.

"Thanks for being so generous."

"We're raising a generation that has grown up with constant connection. They don't know how to be alone. For them, being alone means not being connected. If you don't learn how to be truly alone, you'll always be lonely."

"Believe me, I know how to be alone. And lonely. At the same time even."

"Loneliness is absolute," Jessica states.

"That's so dismal."

"It's interesting how people these days mistake sharing an idea for having the original idea. It's not, 'I think, therefore I am.' Now it's, 'I share, therefore I am.' For some, the simulated experience is as real as the actual experience," Jessica adds.

"It's a generation of simulators. A plague of plagiarists."

"We're encouraged to live more and more of our lives 'simulating' real life."

"Imitation is the sincerest form of flattery. I admire, therefore I copy."

"You know what I think constantly being connected means to people?" Jessica asks.

"Please share."

"It represents hope and change and the new. The possible. Anything could happen. Things can be what they aren't now. Better even. I think we all want that."

"Why wouldn't we?"

"To paraphrase Sylvester the cab driver in *The Bishop's Wife* …"

Melissa rolls her eyes.

"'People don't know where they're going, and they want to get there too fast.' Let's slow down and figure out where we're going."

On her way to the shop, Jessica walks through the Julio and Aileen Gallo Rose Garden. She notices an abandoned bicycle with training wheels lying on its side. She stoops to right it. She sees the bright shiny spokes. She cries.

Chapter 7

The drifting fog muffles the neon sign of Galletto Ristorante. Inside, the Mud Bowl banquet is in full swing. Framed photos, tarnished trophies, and ragged T-shirts from past games lie scattered around the room. The party favors are equal parts Mud Bowl nostalgia, high school reunion, and birthday celebration.
One group of older men in their early forties, better known as "The Dinosaurs," sit on one side of a U-shaped table.

Another group of men in their late thirties, known as "The Youngbloods," sit on the opposite side.

More alcohol than food litters the tables.

The origin of the Mud Bowl is cloudy. It depends on who you ask. One participant will say it started in the junior year of high school of Michael's class. Another classmate will say it began their freshman or junior year of college, when the players came home from school for Thanksgiving.

One thing everyone agrees on is that it involved the merging of two groups of high school friends, who had been playing football over the years in two separate locations. One at Pike Park, the other at Roosevelt Junior High School. When the two groups combined, the game moved to Thousand Oaks Park near Dry Creek. Everyone vowed that the game would last as long as there were two players standing. Or leaning.

Trophies had been awarded from the beginning to honor the players who had a good game. Photos and commemorative T-shirts were added along the way. Alcohol had also been there from day one. The banquet had been initiated when an acquaintance of one of the players had told him about a similar tradition held in Buffalo, New York. The players decided it would be a nice way to kick off the holiday weekend.

Michael hunkers down with the "old farts." His thirty-eight-year old younger brother, Daniel Rivers, Jr., hangs with the "new kids."

Sitting beside the two groups of men are wives, girlfriends, and significant others. Michael is the exception. He's flying solo tonight.

An expensive bottle of California wine rests on a side table. Propped against it is a card that reads: "The Last Mud Bowler." In a somber mood likely fueled by too much alcohol and too little sleep, the Bowlers had come up with the idea of having the last man standing pop the cork and toast his departed gladiators.

At the top of the "U," a video clip flickers on a television monitor. The song Jessica recorded plays through the set of speakers aligned on each side of the monitor. The images on the screen include shots of the men in this room – these "Boys of Winter" – through the years, playing football in the rain and mud. The electronic images bathe the room in blue light. No one stirs. Everyone is mesmerized.

The last drinks are finished. The handshakes and hugs exchanged. The final taunts hurled. The players and significant others drift into the mist.

Michael and Jessica linger at the back of the room.

He reaches out and squeezes her shoulder.

Jessica smiles and touches the pin he gave her. She turns to leave.

"Be careful out there. The fog is thick as mud."

"I'll keep both eyes open, both hands on the wheel."

"I don't enjoy visiting hospitals."

Chapter 8

Thanksgiving Day dawns on Legion Park. Hundreds of runners, young and old, prepare for this year's Turkey Trot, Gobbler Walk, and Kids Run. The costumes are as creative as the participants are diverse.

Jessica is dressed as a Pilgrim. She wears a fabric turkey on her head. Melissa is dressed as a Native American. She wears a fabric cornucopia. The thundering herd sprints through the drizzle. The sisters walk in their wake.

At her house later that morning, Jessica and Melissa, still dressed in their Gobbler costumes, watch the Macy's Thanksgiving Day parade. They snack on pumpkin pie.

"I hope Santa is sober," Jessica says.

"If he isn't, they'll have a hard time finding Edmund Gwen."

"I'd love to be in New York."

"Why can't you be happy with where you are?" Melissa asks.

"It's the place to be at Christmas."

"That's so you. If you're on an adventure, you

want to be home. If you're home, you want to be on an adventure. It's never Goldilocks with you. Nothing is ever just right."

"Christmas in New York is the best. Josh and I loved it."

"An old boyfriend. An old memory. Don't turn it into something it isn't. Or never was."

"The Rockettes at Radio City, lighting the tree at Rockefeller Center, Times Square, St. Patrick's Cathedral, Saks Fifth Avenue, a snow-covered Central Park, visiting Macy's and seeing where Edmund Gwen sat when they were filming *Miracle on 34th Street*. I'll never forget those moments."

"Or the police armed with automatic weapons," Melissa reminds her little sister.

"It's a different world now."

"They win if we don't show up."

"We can't let that happen."

"No, we can't."

They toast with their slices of pumpkin pie.

"Maybe it's the season," Jessica continues. "Or seeing the nativities each day. Maybe it's hearing the carols. Whatever it is, I think more and more about religion this time of year."

"There is something comforting about the essence of religion."

"Things like love, peace, and forgiveness.

Compassion, charity, and atonement. Acceptance and gratitude."

"All good things to live by," Melissa says.

"Now and again, I wonder what it would be like to surrender to faith. To let someone else be in control. Someone else be responsible. Make the hard calls. To feel safe and comfortable knowing that living a spiritual life will lead to something better. Some day."

"I don't see you as the surrendering kind."

"Not generally."

"Plus, you don't need religion for that," Melissa adds. "You can find the spiritual in nature, community service, the arts. All kinds of things that can soothe the soul."

"Everyday things."

"*The Bible* is a wonderful story," Melissa continues. "An inspirational collection of myths and teachings."

"But, it doesn't work for everyone."

"Do you believe?"

"In a higher power?"

"Or something."

"I do. I'm not sure what it is."

"Neither do I."

"Buddha was not a Buddhist," Jessica replies. "Jesus was not a Christian. Muhammed was not a Muslim. They were teachers who taught love."

"Love was their religion."

"By whatever name He is called, He personifies the spirit of loving and giving."

"And peace and mercy, which we certainly could use more of," Melissa observes.

"That's why I collect so many nativities. That's the heart of Christmas for me. A child. A journey. A mother's love. A celebration."

"Unfortunately, there are those who turn that love inside out. Who do awful things in the name of religion."

"I will never understand that. How can you kill someone in the name of your God, whoever or whatever that may be?"

"It's been going on since man started believing in a higher power than himself."

"It's truly hard to believe."

They both gaze at the parade winding through New York.

"Shall we go see what mischief the mud boys are getting into?" Melissa asks.

"We shall."

Chapter 9

Raindrops pelt a puddle of water in the middle of Thousand Oaks Park. The Dinosaurs and Youngbloods arrive alone and in small groups, with family and friends. Each wears the same "uniform" they've worn every year. Now tattered, torn, and too many sizes too small.

The local news media descends. Two TV crews. A newspaper reporter and his photographer. The reporters set up and begin interviewing players and observers. One of the reporters is an attractive woman. The guys wrestle to be the first in line to talk with her.

Ice chests are filled and brown bags removed, as most of the players suck on a collection of alcoholic beverages, puff on cigarettes, or simply hang out and catch up.

Flags are passed out and cinched over bellies five times the size of the school kids who normally wear them.

Some of the players try to hold their weary and worn bodies together with athletic tape and an assortment of ankle, knee, and wrist braces.

Parents, brothers, sisters, children, wives, and lovers appear and set up lawn chairs and blankets in the same location they do each year. Everywhere, dogs and kids scurry underfoot.

On the sidelines and the field of play, the players go through pre-game rituals. A couple half-heartedly run patterns, catch passes, and kick punts.

Arrayed on the ground is the collection of iron: Individual trophies for MVP, "Best O," and "Best D," as well as the "Cheap Shot" rubber chicken and the commemorative plaque listing past game results and trophy winners.

Representatives for each team walk off the boundaries, marking end zones and first downs with orange traffic cones. They argue as they go. The squabbling sounds like a schoolyard light years ago.

Down at one end of the field, another game has already begun. Between the children of these "boys," as they prepare for the day when they will take up the gauntlet from their fathers.

Following the kickoff, Michael and Dan, Jr. face each other on opposite sides of the line of scrimmage.

Jessica and Melissa watch from the sidelines. Melissa shoots photos with her digital camera and an old Polaroid camera, which Jessica gave her last Christmas.

The game starts slowly and badly for the old dudes. They can't seem to move the ball.

The new kids march up and down the field at will, scoring two quick touchdowns.

A teacher's test clock dings, signaling the end of the first half.

Watching the boys jostle and josh each other while trudging off the field, Jessica thinks, *My family loves nicknames. We give them to each other, to relatives, to friends, even strangers. Dad was known as "Tooter," for his clarinet and saxophone playing in high school. Mom was known as "Dynamite," for being who she was. Michael is "Mikey," "Mickey," or "Riv," which was shorthand for Rivers. Dan, Jr. is "D-Honey" and "Bone Sights, Jr." Johnny was "Spindle Fibers," "Harry Joe Brown," or "J-Stoner," which was shortened to "Stoner" and took on different implications as he grew up and became a musician. Melissa is "Mel," "Lisa," or "Mello." My nicknames include "Jess" or "Ick."*

Michael in particular loves conferring nicknames. His old buddy Allen was "Jorge," which was Spanish for his middle name. His college buddies were "Gover," "Wally Gator," "the Red Herring," and "the Mudcat."

His fellow "Mud Bowlers" have taken nicknaming to a whole different level. The Bowlers all have appropriate, personalized monikers, immortalized in each year's banquet video. In addition to Mikey, D-Honey, and Jorge, there is Si, Bo'Re, Goat, Hands, Scur, Vanston and Lanston, Kipling, Big Cou and Little Cou, Stein, Hollywood, Pancho, Big Boy, Dancing Bear, Roy Boy, Fast Johnnie, Hoden, Putz, and Henniputz.

As the Bowlers mix and mingle, Jessica muses, *If we gave you a nickname, that meant you were accepted into the clan. It was our way of controlling our world. If we could name it, we could claim it.*

During halftime, the players head for chairs and significant others. And continue to drink. Some try to catch their breath or walk off pulled muscles. The reporters swoop in again.

Michael and Dan, Jr. limp off the field and stand next to their siblings. Joining the four siblings are Dan, Jr.'s wife, Linda, and their two sons, fifteen-year-old Jared and thirteen-year-old Travis. Both are covered in mud from running through the puddles in their game, the same as their father and uncle.

Michael looks up at the road above the park.

Jessica follows his gaze. She sees a woman standing at the top of the stairs leading down to the park.

"She ever going to join us?" Jessica asks. "We ever going to actually meet her?"

"Rachael's intimidated by you all," Michael answers.

"We're not that bad."

"We're a tough nut to crack."

Michael waves to the woman.

Rachael Giddings waves back, then walks across the street to her car.

"Why wasn't she there last night?"

"Same reason."

"Too bad. She'll never get to know us if she doesn't get to know us," Dan, Jr. adds.

"It's days like this I really miss Mom and Dad," Michael says, turning back to the field and looking at the people standing in clumps on the sidelines.

"And Johnny," Melissa adds.

"They never missed a game," Dan, Jr. says.

"This time of year, in particular, we think about them," Jessica comments.

"And the others we've lost," says Dan, Jr.

"How many players are gone?" Melissa asks.

"A couple. Kevin, Don, and Brad," Michael answers.

"And you're best bud, Allen," Jessica adds.

"That's more than a couple," Melissa says.

"Sad to say, it is," responds Dan, Jr.

"I'm tired of losing people," Michael continues.

"I was sorry to hear about Chris," Melissa tells Michael.

"I wasn't ready for that one," Michael answers.

"We never are," adds Dan, Jr.

"They're all here. In some way," Jessica says

Michael reacts with a glance that says, "What are you smoking?"

"I believe that, too," Melissa defends her sister.

"You and Allen sure could harmonize," Michael tells Jessica.

"He was easy to sing with."

"You two made the Bowl videos special," Michael adds.

"With a little help from middle brother Johnny," Jessica answers.

"Speaking of missing," Michael comments. "I thought Josh planned on playing this year."

"And Brandon," Dan, Jr. adds.

"No show at the banquet," Michael says. "Then today. I'm beginning to think they don't like us."

"Brandon was going to play," Jessica defends her fiancé. "But he was afraid he might run into Josh."

"Concerned your ex-boyfriend might cheap shot him?" Michael asks.

"Something mildly macho like that," Jessica answers.

"And Josh? What was his alibi?" Dan, Jr. asks.

"Thought Brandon would be here."

"That's the problem with inviting boyfriends," Dan, Jr. continues. "Can't count on 'em."

Jessica punches her next oldest brother's arm.

"Since Josh didn't make it either, it was much ado about nothing," Michael says.

"They wouldn't have done anything anyway," Jessica answers.

"Oh, to have two knights jousting over you on the field of battle. A dream come true," Melissa pines.

"Too bad. We could use them both right now," Dan, Jr. says.

"You guys don't need more players. You need a doctor," Michael ribs.

Michael playfully pokes his younger brother in the gut.

"Brandon had to take care of some out-of-town business," Jessica explains.

"Nothing says a family holiday like taking care of business in another city," Michael accuses.

"Will we see him at Christmas?" Melissa asks.

"Maybe," Jessica replies.

"Doesn't sound promising," Dan, Jr. observes.

"It's no big deal."

"Too bad," Michael responds. "I sort of like him."

"Me, too," Jessica says.

"You should be more like him," Michael adds.

The game is over. The trophies awarded. The "boys of winter" say their "goodbyes" and "catch you next years." The cones and flags are collected. The Mud Bowl commemorative plaque is propped against a tree. Taped to the face is the final score. The Dinosaurs beat The Youngbloods "Six Touchdowns to Five." A Polaroid group portrait of the players rests against the plaque. In the photo, Michael holds his "Best Offense" trophy and Dan, Jr. cradles "Best Defense."

Chapter 10

On her way to the bank on Friday, Jessica stops at the McHenry Mansion visitor center and gift shop. Located in a smaller building adjacent to the mansion, the visitor center includes historical photos and a DVD history of the mansion. Tours of the mansion begin here. The gift store sells books, Christmas ornaments, collectibles, and artwork. Jessica donates copies of her music, art, and books to benefit the mansion foundation. Today, she is checking to see if anything needs to be restocked for the Christmas season. It doesn't.

Leaving the visitor center, she walks by the stately and beautifully decorated Victorian home. As she passes the stairs that descend to a basement entrance, she hears a whimpering. She retraces her steps to the stairs. Huddled against the freezing cold is a five-year-old girl with no jacket or blanket.

Jessica steps down the stairs.

"Are you okay?" she asks.

No answer. Only the sound of chattering teeth.

"Where are your parents?" she asks again.

"Gone. Maybe jail."

"Where's your home?"

"I dunno. Sometimes here, sometimes our car.

Anywhere we can."

"Come with me."

"Where?" the young girl asks.

"Someplace safe."

"I'm safe here."

"Somewhere warm, then. With food. And hot chocolate."

"Really?"

"Really."

"Okay."

The girl rises. Jessica wraps the girl in her coat.

Inside the kitchen of the nearby First Methodist Church, the girl blows on her steaming chocolate.

Jessica waits next to Mary, an older member of the congregation, who also sings in the choir.

"She seems better already," Jessica observes.

"All she needs is some food and a mother's love and she'll be fit as a fiddle," Mary says.

Jessica reacts, frowning as Mary's comment conjures up a memory. Jessica glances first at the child then at the nativity sitting on a side table.

"Let me know what you find out," Jessica replies.

"I will. She's lucky you saw her. I'm not sure how much longer she would have lasted out there."

It's an exciting evening when Santa Claus comes to

town. He arrives at McHenry Village in a little red deuce coupe pulled by two Tule elk. The deuce coupe in honor of Modesto's *American Graffiti* heritage and the Tule elk in acknowledgement of the animals native to the Central Valley.

Jessica and Melissa are there for St. Nick's arrival, dressed in knockoffs of the Christmas gowns worn by Rosemary Clooney and Vera-Ellen in Irving Belin's *White Christmas*. They wave to Santa and cheer, along with dozens of other shoppers.

"Look at those faces," Jessica says, as she points at the row of smiling youngsters.

"That used to be us," Melissa says.

"A long time ago."

"Not so long ago."

"I can't believe Thanksgiving has come and gone already," Jessica laments.

"Who knows where the time goes."

A sadness crosses Jessica's face.

"Why so down?" Melissa asks.

"Reminded me of something."

"Or someone."

"I suppose."

"How old would she have been?"

"Five. It goes by so fast."

"Too fast."

"I wish I could hold back the hands of time."

"There you go again," Melissa teases. "Getting all introspective."

"Sorry. Old habits die hard."

"We've got a bunch of good years ahead of us."

"I hope," Jessica replies.

"Lighten up, my dear."

"I'll blame it on the boys."

"They deserve it."

"All their talk of people gone too soon got me thinking."

"About?"

"Mortality. How quickly it's all gone."

"Doom. Doom. You sound like a funeral bell tolling," Melissa says. "Enough with the gloom. All the more reason to live the best life possible right now."

"If the fates allow."

Where did the time go? Jessica thinks to herself. *Who knew. Thoughts about time passing quickly often came to her with the change of seasons, a birthday, a holiday, seeing someone she hadn't seen in some time, when she sang Judy Collins' Who Knows Where the Time Goes?, or as now, when she thought of someone she'd lost. This question nearly always recalls a poem by Dr. Seuss, "How did it get so late so soon? It's night before it's afternoon. December is here before it's June. My goodness how the time has flewn. How did it get so late so soon?"*

As she grows older, it feels like time passes more

quickly than when she was younger, not that she's that old now. She recalls her parents speaking of how it seemed time moved faster the older they got. Her father had often said we shouldn't lament what we missed, what we didn't do. We should instead celebrate what we experienced, what we did do. Jessica has a hard time doing that because time is hard for her.

For her, and others like her, it is always about time. Slipping away. Being wasted. Running out. Standing still. Flying. Being lost. Filling, making, and killing it. Or, having enough of it. She and her contemporaries worry about it being the last time, or the last time around. It is always time to do this, or that. We think about time zones, time outs, and real time – just in time or the nick of time or putting in time. We tell stories about once upon a time and share proverbs about a stitch in time. We fondly recall the first time and agonize over the only time. We try to take things one step at a time. We long for the time when time was on our side.

Time and again, we talk about prime time, big time, me or my time, good time, nap time, in time, alone time, night-time, hang time, Christmas time, every time, lost time, quiet time, any time, wintertime, sleepy time, strange time, short-time, part-time, all-time, the right and wrong time. We read Time Magazine or the New York Times, Of Time and the River, or The Time Machine. We nostalgically look back at the times of our life and hope we had the time of our life. We set our clocks to

*Greenwich Mean Time and Pacific Standard Time. From
time to time, we ponder time management, which we
got around to when we had time, and time travel which
inevitably requires a time machine. We imagine what
having time on our hands, or the end of time, actually
looks like. We question if there is world enough and time.
We sing "The times they are a-changin'," "Time is on
my side," "Time has come today," and "By the time I get
to Phoenix." We often don't have time to take our time.
We ask, what came first, life or time? As one Brainiac
pointed out, "if it weren't for time, everything would
happen all at once at the same time." And, finally, there
comes a time when we discover that Father Time waits
for no one.*

*The older we get, the less there seems to be of it and
the faster it goes. Something we think took place two
years ago is actually five or ten. And we insist on rushing
toward then without living in the now, this moment. Only
to look back and wonder why we are in such a hurry for
the arrival of tomorrow when today will soon enough be
gone to yesterday. It has been said that yesterday is the
past, tomorrow is the future, but today is a gift and that's
why it's called the present.*

*In the romantic comedy movie, "About Time," a
young man named Tim learns from his father that the
men in their family have the ability to travel back in
time. Not forward, just back, which provides our hero
with the opportunity to change his past so he can have*

*a better future. Near the end of the movie, Tim learns
that his father has terminal cancer, which cannot be
changed by time travel. When Tim reels back in time
to visit his father the day before he is to be buried, his
father counsels him to live each day twice. The first time
to experience it in real time as it happens with all the
stresses a "normal" person faces. And a second time,
now knowing what to expect from the day, in order to
savor each moment; embracing the day and enjoying it
for exactly what it is. Like a good son, Tim follows his
father's advice. But, he soon realizes that it is a far, far
better thing to live each day once and enjoy it as if it
were his last.*

Jessica can't help but chuckle as her thoughts are
interrupted by a quote from Groucho Marx, *"Time flies
like an arrow; fruit flies like a banana."*

The Sonora Craft Fair and Music Festival takes place
each year over Thanksgiving weekend at the Sonora
Fairgrounds. Sonora is a gold rush town located in the
foothills above Modesto.

Jessica's mother was born in a tiny town near Sonora
named Stent. She was one of fourteen children. She
lived in a wooden shack with no electricity or indoor
plumbing. They were California hillbillies. She couldn't
wait to fly the coop. Jessica's dad was happy to help.

Jessica's mom and dad were introduced by a friend
of her mom's, who happened to be her dad's cousin.
Jessica's dad was back in Manteca after coming home
from World War II. They met in Strawberry, a small
town in the Sierra foothills above Sonora, where her
mother was working at the snack bar of the local store
and her dad was working a timber crew and tooling
around on his Indian motorcycle. They continued seeing
one another when Jessica's mom got a job working
as a telephone operator in Stockton and Jessica's dad
arranged for her to room in a boarding house owned by
his aunt. He, too, would soon start working for Ma Bell.
It was a short courtship. They married at Stockton's City
Hall. Michael was born a year later.

Jessica's mom was incredible. She raised five kids
in a small house. She cooked, she cleaned, she drove
her children everywhere. She protected and defended
them. Heaven help anyone who attacked, or demeaned,
her flock. She welcomed their friends and created an
extended family.

Jessica smiles at the image of her mother, the mother
hen, as the flurry of the craft fair swirls around her.

The festival features over 150 artisans, musical
acts, street performers, costumed Christmas characters,
carolers, and food. This year's event is somewhat
somber because it will be the last.

Jessica sits inside her vendor booth. She's dressed in
a replica of the gown worn by Vera-Ellen in the "Sisters"

scene from *White Christmas*. Arrayed behind her is her artwork. In addition to her Christmas work, she does watercolor and acrylic abstracts of Modesto and the Central Valley. Spread across the table in front of her are her music cassettes, which feature original songs about her home town. Her children's Christmas books are also on display, each of which take place in Modesto and the valley. Judging from the quality of the work and the number of buyers, she's a triple crown winner. Jessica sketches some of the craft fair participants and visitors.

Melissa, who has been wandering the miles of aisles, stops at her sister's booth to check in. She's dressed in a recreation of the gown worn by Rosemary Clooney in the same "Sisters" scene from *White Christmas*.

"When are you performing?" Melissa asks.

"At 4."

"Not a bad time slot."

"After Sourdough Slim."

"Tough act to follow."

"Magnolia Rhythm Trio after me. I feel like an 'Americana' sandwich."

"Any of the cousins stop by?" Melissa asks.

"Not yet."

"It'd be great to see them more."

"We could try harder, I guess."

"Mom made it tough."

"Once she was gone, she never looked back."

"All those kids."

"A rattle-trap shed for a home."

"With an outhouse."

"Can you imagine?" Jessica says.

"Can't blame her."

"No wonder she hated camping."

"We thought we were better than them."

"No way to treat family."

Two teenaged sisters dressed as Elsa and Anna from *Frozen* stop to admire a sketch Jessica did of them. The young girls inspire Jessica and Melissa to re-enact the "Sisters" dance routine from *White Christmas.*

"'*Sisters, sisters,*'" Jessica and Melissa sing. "'*There were never such devoted sisters. Lord help the mister, who comes between me and my sister. And lord help the sister, who comes between me and my man.*'"

Chapter 11

Back in town later that Saturday, Jessica's hectic holiday continues at ModShop, a craft fair hosted by Modesto's downtown merchants. Artisans sell their handmade goods. Musicians entertain the browsers. The restaurants overflow with diners.

The downtown is hopping with shopping. Locals enjoy the festive scene of music, delicious food, tasty drink, and community.

The Mistlin Art Gallery is jammed with artists, lookers, and buyers. Attendees check out the handmade goods, visit with friends, and sample the appetizers and libations.

In one corner, Jessica sits behind her wooden card table. Her artwork, audiocassettes, and books are displayed. Jessica accepts some money, writes a receipt, places the merchandise in a recyclable bag, and thanks the purchaser, who steps aside to reveal Josh Patterson, Jessica's thirty-year-old ex-boyfriend, and Savannah Marlow, his twenty-something girlfriend.

"Happy Holidays, Jessica," Josh greets Jessica.

"Merry Christmas, Josh," Jessica replies, casting a glance at Savannah.

"Jessica Rivers, this is Savannah Marlow. Savannah,

this is Jessica," Josh makes the introductions.

Savannah nods and smiles.

Jessica comes around the table and hugs her.

"You'll need that," she says, before returning to sit behind her table.

"Always taking the high road," Josh comments.

"Always. My brothers wanted you to know they missed you at the Mud Bowl."

"We were at Savannah's folks."

"Maybe next year."

"Of course. There's always next year."

"You must be a good influence," Jessica says to Savannah.

"Why's that?" Savannah asks.

"He never did his Christmas shopping until Christmas Eve."

"Which reminds me," Josh answers. "I'd like a couple of your books."

"Who should I make them out to?"

"Not sure yet. How about leaving that part blank?"

"For now," Savannah says.

"Absolutely. Inscription 'blank' for now."

"Sounds semi-serious," a male voice says.

They all turn to see thirty-one-year-old Brandon Johnson, Jessica's fiancé.

"Hey Brandon," Josh says. "It's been a while."

Josh and Brandon exchange an awkward "brother" handshake.

"It has," Brandon replies. "I guess we're in trouble with the Rivers boys for not making the game."

"That's what I hear."

"They're big boys," Brandon says. "They'll get over it."

"Absolutely."

Brandon turns to Savannah and extends a hand.

"Brandon Johnson. I'm with her," he says, pointing at Jessica.

Brandon and Savannah shake hands. He turns on the charm. She's affected, as most women are when they meet Brandon.

"We've done what we've come to do, so I think we'll check out the rest of the shops. Wonderful to see you, Jess," Josh says.

"You, too. Nice to meet you, Savannah."

"Yes, lovely," Savannah replies.

"Take care, Brandon," Josh adds, with a smile.

"See you around," Brandon replies, with a scowl.

Josh and Savannah disappear into the crowd.

"That was awkward," Brandon observes.

"I didn't think so."

"Is he still doing that organic thing? Wine or something, I think you said."

"We didn't get to that but, yes, that's the latest."

"Good for him."

"It is. And for the planet."

"Of course. Of course." Brandon checks his phone.

"What time do you think you'll wrap up here?"

"I've got another few hours."

"Serious? You can't cut out early?"

"Not really. As you can see, it's going well. You wouldn't leave a sales presentation before it's time, would you?"

"I suppose not."

A long line of shoppers waits patiently behind Brandon, who doesn't seem to notice or care. He picks up a cassette. On the cover is a black and white photo of the Mud Bowlers from some long-ago decade. The title reads: "The Greatest Hits of the Mud Bowl."

"These selling well?" he asks.

"Not bad."

"They should. You're as good as most."

"Thank you, Brandon."

"I mean it. I wish you knew it."

"I'm getting there."

"You splitting the profits with Michael?"

"All mine."

"Big of him."

"Why do you do that?"

"What?"

"Run him down. He likes you."

"I like him, too."

"So … ?"

"He takes advantage of you. Thanksgiving rolls

around and he expects you to record a song for his latest opus."

"I enjoy it. I like all the guys. It allows me to spend time with him. And them."

"And not me."

"It's not a competition."

"All I know is, he couldn't do it without you."

"I doubt that."

Brandon gives her a look. His cell phone rings.

"I've got to take this. Besides, your public awaits."

Brandon pushes his way through the crowd.

The exclusive gated community of Fleur de Lis is located in the northwest part of town. It's a newer development of custom homes, including Brandon's. The outside of his house is an imposing, Italianate façade, while the interior is large, comfortable, and well-ordered. He has completely "teched" the halls.

Brandon savors a martini, Jessica a Tom & Jerry. Her drink was a choice of her mother and father's generation. It has fallen out of favor with the Millennials.

"How did you do?" Brandon asks.

"It was a particularly good night."

"Terrific."

"It was nice seeing those merry faces downtown."

"Consumers consuming."

"It's more than that. It's community."

"I'm sure the Chamber of Commerce was thrilled."

Jessica scans the house. It is completely bare of any Christmas decorations

"Your decorations aren't up," she observes.

"It's early."

"It might liven things up a bit."

"I like it like this."

"Even a tiny tree would help," she says, as she pulls a small artificial tree from her voluminous handbag and sets it on the coffee table. "There, isn't that better?"

"Here we go."

"What?"

"Just like clockwork."

"What is?"

"You set yourself up."

"For what?"

"You have this Capracorn-Baileyish-Rockwellian expectation of what the holidays should be. A picture-perfect illusion created by movies, TV, books, and social media."

"I don't do social media."

"Whatever. You compare yourself and what your Christmas is like to what other people's Christmases are like. You imagine everybody else is having a better time."

"I'm a Californian. That's what we do."

"It's not real."

"Leave my illusions alone. What have they ever done to you?"

"The more realistic you are about the true meaning of the holidays, the better off you'll be."

"And what's that?"

"It's about consumption, money, and wretched excess, not celebration or togetherness, not even perfection or innocence."

"But, that's why I love Christmas. I can be a child again. I don't have to act like an adult. I have no cares. No obligations. I can escape to ChristmasLand."

"Grow up."

"I'm Peter Pan. Here in Califia, we don't have to."

"That's not realistic."

"That's peachy by me."

"Each and every year, you hope – you expect – that the holidays will make up for the problems that exist the rest of the year. That it will all work out. That it will be a time of loving forgiveness and joyful reunion."

"It can be."

"It's a myth. The season magnifies everything we're missing. The people, the things, the emotions."

"I know that. It's hard, but I get it."

"All that grief and loss. It's made worse."

"It's my way of remembering what's gone."

"That's why so many people go for the Remy and Remington."

"That's depressing."

"But so very true."

Her eyes glisten with tears. Her lip quivers.

"Okay, okay. I'll keep the tree," he says and leans in to kiss her.

She sneezes.

He jerks back, hoping to avoid the spray.

"You getting a cold?" he asks.

"Maybe."

"I can't afford to get sick."

"Always seems to happen this time of year."

"You're too busy."

"To catch a cold?"

"To stay healthy," he says.

"Being busy doesn't bother me. It keeps my mind off other things."

"Let's not go there now."

"Okay with me."

"You get sick because you're too wrapped up doing things instead of being something."

Jessica winces. That stings.

"You're busy, too," she replies.

"I never see you."

"You're wrong."

"You have no time for me," he complains.

"Wrong again."

"I'm not your priority."

"You are. You just don't see it."

"I wish you were more like our other friends."

"In what way?" Jessica asks.

"Less busy. Less generous. Less involved. Less preoccupied. More ... Motherly."

That last word hits her like a punch to the stomach.

"Stop 'Frankensteining' me, Brandon. I am who I am."

"Yes, you are. That may be the problem."

"We've had the talk about children."

"Many, many times."

"I haven't changed my mind."

"I wish we could do something about that."

"Me, too."

It's like a broken record, Jessica thinks to herself. *It always ends this way. He just doesn't understand what it means to lose a child. I'm just not ready yet. I may never be ready.*

Chapter 12

The Sunday service at First Methodist Church is packed with congregants thanks to the long Thanksgiving weekend. Jessica sits with the choir behind the pastor, who delivers his traditional sermon.

"Each of us has a special gift to give to each other, our community, and ourselves, especially at this time of year. What is yours? Compassion, charity, or hope? Perhaps forgiveness or generosity? These are the shining gifts that bring us peace on earth. There are so many lonely people out there whose stocking is empty. It is in each of us to bring them comfort and joy. In helping them, we show that we care more about our neighbors than we care about ourselves. Our life can truly be about the lives we touch. For good. No one is forgotten who eases the pain of others. That is the true gift of Christmas. What special gift do you want to give to the world?"

After the service, the choir rehearses for this year's Christmas Pageant. They sing "Bells of Christmas."

Jessica loves every minute of it. She gets to sing songs about Christmas.

Following rehearsal, Jessica exits the front door of the

church and walks toward her parked VW bus.

As she opens the car door, a ten-year-old homeless boy with a limp approaches her. His legs are supported by an iron frame. He leans on a crutch.

"Spare change?" he asks.

Jessica is bewildered and saddened by what she sees. She rummages in her shoulder bag, removes some change, and hands it to him.

He offers her a white lily and a red rose. She takes them.

"Pretty," he says.

"They are."

"They're a lot like us."

"Really? How?" Jessica asks.

"Unlike us, flowers have no memory. No thoughts of the past or future. They live in the present. Only for today. Simply to share their beauty."

"Sounds similar to something someone said to me not long ago."

"Have you ever watched a river flow?"

"I have."

"When you look up river, then look at where you're standing, then look down river, it's as if the past, present, and future are streaming right before your eyes. You learn from yesterday, live for today, and hope for tomorrow."

"Everything is connected, isn't it," Jessica says. She smells the flowers.

"Thanks for the change."

The boy tucks the money in his pocket and leaves Jessica standing by the open car door.

On the television in the sun porch of Jessica's house, the end credits roll for the movie, *Holiday Inn*. Watching are Jessica, Melissa, Dan, Jr., and Michael. Just the sibs. The coffee and side tables are laden with snacks and drinks. A stack of VHS tapes towers beside the TV set. It includes almost every Christmas movie ever made, including such gems as *Santa Claus Conquers the Martians* with Pia Zadora.

"Well, that's another traditional Rivers' family Christmas movie marathon in the books," Melissa observes.

"Thanks for organizing," Dan, Jr. says to Jessica.

"It's what I do best."

"I'm sorry Rachael couldn't join us," Melissa says.

"How is she?" Jessica asks.

"Tentative," Michael answers.

"She'll come around," Jessica replies.

"I hope."

"We can be intimidating," Dan, Jr. adds.

"No kidding."

"With the marathon done, I've got a new one," Melissa says.

"There's not enough days in the calendar for all the holiday traditions you two have come up with," Michael complains.

"Humbug!" his younger siblings chime in as one.

Melissa sets a large, poster-shaped package covered with Christmas wrapping paper on the arms of an easy chair.

"As some of you may know, the 'Countdown to Christmas' on the Hallmark Channels has started."

Michael groans. Everyone else applauds.

"The first one aired right before Halloween," Melissa adds.

"That's sick," Michael says.

"No, that's Hallmark," replies Dan, Jr.

"So, when I was Googling the movie schedule, something popped up that caught my eye," Melissa continues. "A woman in Fort Worth, Texas, posted this on Facebook."

With a flourish, Melissa removes the wrapping paper. At the top of the poster, she has hand-written: "Hallmark Drinking Game."

"Ta da! I give you the 'Hallmark Christmas Drinking Game'."

More hoots and hand-clapping.

Below the title, the poster lists the number of drinks to be taken for each of the predictable incidents that happen in a Hallmark movie. For example, "Take a Drink ..." any time there is a "Reference to a dead relative." Take two if there is a "Near miss kiss." Take three "When the family business takeover is thwarted." And so on.

"Now this is a Christmas tradition I can get into," Michael says.

"The tree isn't all that's getting lit today," Dan, Jr. adds.

"The rules are pretty self-explanatory," Melissa points out, drawing her finger down the list. "You take one drink if any of these things happen." She points at the next items on the list. "Two if you see any of these." She points one more time and says, "And three for these. You must finish your drink 'When the cynic is filled with the Christmas spirit,' or 'When it snows on Christmas.'"

"What if it snows in the Central Valley?" Jessica asks.

"That never happens," Dan, Jr. replies.

"When hell freezes over," Michael grumbles.

"There's also a bonus," Melissa continues. "You have to take a shot if the movie features Candace Cameron-Bure or Lacey Chabert."

"I don't know those people," Michael says.

"Sure, you do," Jessica points out.

"You'll recognize them as soon as you see them," Dan, Jr. says.

Melissa checks her watch. "Okay, it's almost time. Everyone have a full glass?"

"Yes, Melissa," Jessica and Dan, Jr. reply together.

They all look at Michael.

"Yes, Melissa," he answers.

"Ladies and gentlemen, start your engines."

Jessica flips on the TV. Melissa flops down on the couch. The music swells and the opening credits appear over a beautiful, snowy landscape.

Jessica, Melissa, and Dan, Jr. cheer and take a sip.

"I'm just here to drink," Michael says.

"Then this game's for you," Dan, Jr. responds.

Michael takes a long drink and pours another one.

In the first scene of the movie, the main character is played by Lacey Chabert, she's named Holly, and she's drinking chocolate.

"That's a triple off the center field wall right out of the gate," Melissa chuckles.

Everyone takes three drinks.

Michael keeps chugging.

"You're not playing it right, Melissa says. "All you're doing is drinking."

Michael toasts her and drinks.

"You're no fun," Melissa says.

"I'm the 'no fun' guy."

"Buckle up, it's going to be a tipsy night," Jessica observes.

Each Christmas season for as long as she can remember, Jessica has taken the time to reach out during the holidays, sharing her love of the season through her many talents.

She plays music for the residents of the Senior Center.

There was never a moment of rest this time of year, Jessica muses to herself.

Jessica reads one of her children's Christmas books to sick children at the local children's hospital.

I wanted everyone to feel the same way I did about Christmas.

Jessica teaches disabled children and adults how to paint watercolors.

I wanted the less fortunate and lonely to truly experience this most wonderful time of the year.

Jessica hosts a wreath-making party to benefit the College Area Neighborhood Alliance.

It's a blizzard of activity. She is exhausted. But happy.

I wanted to bring Christmas to life.

Chapter 13

Jessica and Melissa marvel at the bounty spread before them. Jessica is dressed like Loretta Young's character in the movie, *The Bishop's Wife*, ribboned cakebox hat and all. Melissa is costumed as the Grinch. This Christmas banquet is hosted by a fellow musician Michael and Johnny had known since high school. Johnny had played with the host in a couple bands. Early each holiday season, the host invites family, friends, and fellow musicians to break bread and rock out. Johnny and Kristi had performed together many times since it had started. Jessica had joined them from time to time and Melissa sang along a few times. Michael had threatened to learn bass to fill in the missing instrument for the family band, but still hadn't gotten around to it. The food is always incredible. The music is as good, featuring a stellar lineup of players who grew up in Modesto and those who still called Modesto home. Unfortunately, another of the local musicians had recently been diagnosed with cancer. At times like this, the gathering feels more like a wake and less like a celebration.

The two sisters move away from the table with full plates of food and find a place to sit where they can see and hear the music.

"The last time we did this, Johnny was still with us," Melissa says.

"He hadn't looked good."

"He probably shouldn't have been here."

"He was a pro and he was loyal. He had made a commitment and he was going to keep it."

"He never could say no."

"None of us could."

"He really loved playing with all those folks."

"They both did."

"He had never sounded better," Jessica replies. "It was almost as if he knew he had no time left."

"He played like there was no tomorrow which, for him, was true."

Johnny had passed away on the second day in January six years before.

"You two always sounded good together," Melissa says.

"It was in the DNA, I guess. You can't beat coming from the same stock."

"Like the Everly Brothers."

"We could harmonize, but not like those two," Jessica adds.

"I miss him."

"I do, too."

"And Kristi."

"I can't believe they're both gone. It doesn't seem that long ago they were here."

"It's like we've lost a part of us."

"Every day, I want to talk with him about something."

"His smile is what I remember most," Melissa says.

"He was trying so hard to get back in shape."

"A hard road, especially after all those years of being on the road and playing in bars."

"Michael wrote a story about him one time."

"When he was still writing?"

"Yep."

"He was good," Melissa states.

"It was good. He called it 'Trinity'."

Jessica can hear Michael's voice telling the story as she retells it to Melissa.

"I've been fortunate to have three people in my life who I could always talk with about sports, music, and beer. My best friend, Allen, known to some as Jorge, always the joker. My youngest brother, Johnny, better known as Stoner, the rock 'n' roller. And my college buddy, Chris Walsh, AKA Wally Gator, forever the cowboy.

Any time I wanted to catch a game, listen to a song, or sip a cold one, I could count on at least one, and sometimes all three, to be right there with me. The Joker. The Musician. The Cowboy. The wholly and unholy Trinity.

Sadly, the legendary trio is no more. They're all gone. Much too young. Now, conversations about sports, music, and beer are mostly between me, myself, and I.

I created a memorial video for each one. I pored over countless images and tried to select just the right songs to convey the essence of their lives, which, of course, involved sports, music, and beer. It was painful because I realized we wouldn't be making those memories any more. When I finished the tribute to Gator, who was the most recent to leave us, I swore it would be the last. It was just too damned hard. I said adios and happy trails to The Three Amigos.

Until we meet again."

"The Three Amigos."

"Until we meet again," Jessica says.

Jessica and Melissa take their plates into the kitchen and set them on the countertop. Jessica stops as she passes the commercial refrigerator, festooned with "stuff."

"You recall the Christmas you and I toured several homes as part of the 'Holiday Open House' fundraiser for Community Hospice?" Jessica asks.

"I do," replies Melissa. "Each one had refreshments. Some sold home-made gifts. Very festive."

"Every house had its own unique collection of family memorabilia displayed on book shelves, mantles, window sills, pianos, and refrigerators."

"It might've seemed a bit weird," Melissa continues, "but I enjoyed checking out the refrigerators. With their collections of drawings, photos, report cards, coupons, lists, cartoons, reminders, and aspirations."

"Interesting, isn't it?" Jessica says. "A room tells us so much about who we are."

"It is sweet," Melissa adds.

"We display things that are important to us. To prove we're more or less okay. That we make sense. That we have value. That we've been here."

"It is sad."

"The clutter, all the things that are worn out, the things we meant to do, all reveal this brokenness in our lives. Photos, a few trophies, artwork, some rare objects show our pride, our few shining moments."

"Not sure I'd call it 'broken'."

"It's a little selfish," Jessica continues. "We collect all these things, but we're only borrowing them for a while. When we're gone, they go live with somebody else."

"That's depressing."

"These rooms are future ruins."

Melissa gives her little sister that familiar look that says, "Lighten up."

"I remember thinking to myself as we exited one of the homes through the living room, past a piano, a glass display case, and a Christmas tree, 'What will people think when I'm gone and they sift through my ruins? I'm not sure I want to be defined by the artifacts I leave behind.'"

Jessica grew up and went to school with several kids from Jewish families. It was a small community. Allen Mullens' son Dylan had married Carla Grossman, a young Jewish woman from Modesto. Through them, Jessica had become familiar with Hanukkah. Curious and intrigued by the Jewish religion, which she felt was more real, compassionate, nurturing, and forgiving than the religions she was familiar with, she participated in Hanukkah each year.

Hanukkah, which means dedication, commemorates the rededication during the second century B.C. of the Second Temple in Jerusalem, after it was retaken by the Maccabees, a group of Jewish warriors, from their Greek-Syrian oppressors. Hanukkah begins each year on the 25th of Kislev on the Hebrew calendar and usually falls in November or December.

Often called the Festival of Lights, celebrations revolve around the lighting of a nine-branched candelabrum, called a *menorah* or *hanukkiah*. After sundown on each of the holiday's eight nights, another candle is added to the *menorah* and lit until all eight candles are burning on the final night of the festival. A ninth candle in the middle of the *menorah* called the *shammash* ("helper") is used to light the other candles. Jewish families typically recite blessings during this ritual and display the *menorah* prominently in a window or someplace visible as a reminder to others of the miracle that inspired the holiday. The miracle had to do with the fact that, after reclaiming the Temple, there appeared to be only enough untainted olive oil inside the house of worship to burn for one night during the rededication of the temple. But, miraculously, that tiny bit of oil lasted eight days.

In another tradition alluding to the Hanukkah miracle, traditional Hanukkah foods are fried in oil, including potato pancakes (*latkes*) and jam-filled donuts (*sufganiyot*). Other Hanukkah customs involve children playing with four-sided spinning tops called *dreidels* and winning prizes or chocolate coins called *gelt*, the Yiddish word for money. Gifts are often given every night, perhaps due to the influence of Christmas.

Jessica has participated in recent years in the public lighting of the *menorah* hosted by Congregation Beth Shalom, Modesto's synagogue, which was founded in 1918. The ceremony features the lighting of a five-foot-tall *menorah*, the singing of songs, and the sharing of treats. In a past interview in *The Modesto Bee*, Rabbi Shalom Bochner was quoted as saying, "We celebrate Hanukkah at the darkest time of the year by literally adding more light. It may be just a minor holiday, but it has a wonderful, positive message of hope for everyone."

In one more custom involving Hanukkah, Jessica

alternates each year with other friends and family members in the judging of the yearly Grossman family's *latke* cook-off between Carla and her father, Harvey. Carla won for the first time last year and she's hoping to repeat.

For Jessica, the Hanukkah celebrations conjure images from one of her most admired TV shows, *thirtysomething*. In the final scene of the episode entitled "I'll Be Home for Christmas," the protagonist returns home to find his wife, his daughter, and his cousin holding the *shammash*, waiting for him to help light the *menorah*. It was their way of acknowledging that Christmas meant different, equally meaningful things, to Jews and gentiles. Jessica cried every time she saw it.

There are other annual rituals Jessica faithfully practices. Each season, she travels to Columbia State Historical Park in the foothills near Sonora to experience "A Miner's Christmas." The historic gold mining town is decorated for Christmas, as costumed interpreters recreate what a mining camp was really like during the winter months in the 1850s. Homesick miners roast chestnuts, sip hot cider, and perform live music for park visitors. Nineteenth century toys and games, Victorian holiday craft making, and Christmas storytelling offer an enlightening alternative to the holiday craziness. Gathered around the campfire as miners tell tall tales of the gold rush, you might even catch a glimpse of Father Christmas in fur-trimmed buckskin.

Another celebration that occurs nearly every year is the Windham Hill Winter Solstice concert. The Gallo Center toasts the warm traditions of the season by hosting the tour, which features original and traditional acoustic music drawn from the multi-platinum selling *Winter Solstice* series, as well as their many solo releases. The list of performers each year is assembled by Will Ackerman, Windham Hill founder and Grammy-winning guitarist, from a slate of master musicians signed to the record label.

Ackerman founded Windham Hill Records in Palo Alto in 1975. The exceptional quality of the music and recordings were a hit with both critics and audiences. Some of the musicians on the label include Michael Hedges, George Winston, Alex de Grassi, Liz Story, Mark Isham, and Tuck and Patty. Windham Hill's best-selling *Winter Solstice* compilations changed people's perceptions of seasonal music.

Jessica first learned of Windham Hill in college and at home when she listened to KRVR, the local light jazz station. When the company began releasing their collection of holiday songs, Jessica bought the first collection and bought every one that followed.

Although she is an admirer of *The Nutcracker*, as first choreographed and presented by ballet director William Christensen for the San Francisco Ballet, Jessica likes sampling variations on a theme. The San Francisco company had just celebrated their 75th anniversary of being America's first *Nutcracker*. The American premiere of *The Nutcracker* took place on Christmas Eve, 1944, at San Francisco's War Memorial Opera House. It was an instant sensation and launched a national holiday tradition.

One of the more inventive *Nutcrackers* Jessica enjoys is presented by the Dance Brigade's Dance Mission Theater at the Brava Theater in San Francisco. In this unique version of the classic ballet, featuring The Grrrl Brigade and Jr. Grrrl Brigade, Clara is an undocumented worker for the McGreeds, an obscenely wealthy family, and Drosselmeyer is their pink Mohawked, Che-shirt wearing gay son, who presents Clara with a freedom-fighting South African nutcracker. Clara's coming-of-age journey takes her to a world where the Sugar Plum Fairy is homeless and the Snow Queen mourns her melting ice caps. The well-known choreography is supplemented with snippets of aerial work, hip hop, Taiko, belly dance, salsa, and tap. This version of the story inspires us to continue fighting for peace, diversity, and social equality. It is not your grandmother's *Nutcracker* and Jessica loves it.

Chapter 14

Jessica and Michael walk the rows of live Christmas trees. Each is stuck to a piece of rebar embedded in a green plastic basin filled with water. The sign at the gate proclaims, "The Freshest Trees in Town."

"What changed your mind?" Melissa asks.

"The boys. Their mom has one, so I figured I'd better get one to keep up with the Joneses."

"Very in keeping with the season."

"I try. Besides, Rachael wanted one."

"That's an encouraging sign."

Jessica brushes the boughs of potential candidates to see how fresh they really are.

"How tall you thinking?"

"Taller than the ex's."

"Let's make it an even twelve feet."

"Okay."

She leans down to check the base to make sure it's not too big.

"You have a stand that can handle it?"

"I think so."

"You better know so, or you'll be tying it to the fireplace to keep it from flopping over."

"It'll be fine."

"They cross over into a row with taller trees.

"Remember the movie, *The Bishop's Wife*?" Jessica asks.

"How can I forget? You make us watch it every year," Michael answers.

"There's the scene between the Professor and Julia inside Maggenti's flower shop."

"It's etched in my memory. With so many others."

"After haggling with Maggenti over the price per branch, the Professor becomes wistful and says, 'I like to have a Christmas tree because it reminds me of my childhood. I find, for some good reason, that this is a good time of year for looking backward. Can you imagine me ever having been a child?'"

"There's that nostalgia, living in the past thing again."

"Mom was so much the child at Christmas that she had two trees. A living green tree in the family room and an artificial 1960s silver Alcoa in the living room."

"That you now have."

"Each year, when Christmas was over, she would ask Dad to plant the green tree outside the family room window so she could continue to enjoy it until it turned dead brown."

"The rest of the kids in the neighborhood couldn't wait to drag the trees to the curb so they could build tree forts. Us included."

"Mom wanted to hold onto Christmas as long as

she could. The world seemed better. People treated each other more kindly. She wanted desperately to embrace that."

"We all did. Especially Dad."

"You've become Dad, you know. You even look like him."

"That's what people say."

Jessica stares at her older brother. He was Dad. He walked like him. Talked like him. Laughed like him. Had his arms and hands. Chewed like him. Smiled and frowned like him. When he narrowed his eyes and spoke quietly, you knew you were in trouble.

"You strung his old lights in the same way. Staked out an identical flat plastic Santa in his sleigh and eight tiny reindeer on your front lawn. Made his peanut butter chocolate chip cookies and fudge. You had the Alcoa before I did, along with a perfect green tree decorated with old and new ornaments purchased on your trips around the world."

"Until I lost most of them when the boys knocked it over wrestling with each other."

"You played Santa Claus, and tried to keep the truth about Santa from the boys. You ate the cookies they put out."

"I couldn't face another cookie on Christmas morning."

"You assembled something for them or us girls."

"The directions were horrible, usually written by

someone in Taiwan or the Philippines, and the 'toddy for the body' didn't help."

"From bicycles to cardboard kitchens to vanity sets, you and Daddy-O put them together on countless Christmas Eves. As he got older, you did most of it."

"And passed it down to Dan and Johnny."

"Don't forget the 8mm home movies he shot, and you continued. For a while."

"And that crazy light bar it needed. The lights were so bright, every movie featured our family and friends squinting in pain, our hands covering our faces."

"The shots were pretty much the same each year. Up the tree and down the tree. Shots of presents piled under both trees. Close-ups of sleeping animals and passed-out humans. One year, somehow, he double-exposed the film. He must have forgotten that he had already recorded Christmas when he shot a family vacation to SeaWorld. When the film was developed – "

"It featured dolphins and orcas dancing through the Alcoa."

"For me, Christmas is about so many things, like the music."

"And still is."

"I can never get enough of Bing singing 'White Christmas;' Brenda Lee's 'Rockin' Around the Christmas Tree;' 'Run Rudolph Run' by Keith Richards; 'Here Comes Santa Claus' by Gene Autry; or 'Mary, Did You Know?' by Kenny Rogers."

"Or good old Perry 'Coma'."

"And the standards by Percy Faith and John Williams, or *The Nutcracker*."

"Everybody feels compelled to do a Christmas album these days because they sell."

"It's also about the movies. *Holiday Inn, White Christmas, The Bishop's Wife, A Christmas Carol*, and *It's a Wonderful Life*. Over the years, more classics have been added. *The Nutcracker, The Muppet Christmas Carol, National Lampoon's Christmas Vacation, thirtysomething Christmas, The Santa Clause, Scrooged, Home Alone, Love Actually, Elf, A Christmas Story*, and *The Family Stone*."

"All of which you watch every year."

"And the gifts."

"Speaking of crazy."

"We were never wealthy. We had to stand on a ladder to touch the middle class."

"That didn't stop Mom."

"She wanted to make sure we got everything we asked for. Everything. She was born and raised with so little and never forgot it."

"Of course, Dad would spend the rest of the year paying for all the things she ordered."

"One year, I got 42 presents," Jessica says.

"Then you and Johnny would stage your annual who-gets-to-open-the-last-present contest."

"Both of us tucked away at least one present to be

'discovered' after everyone had opened their last gift."

"There were gifts that changed everything. Like the year Johnny got his first guitar and amp. A Sears Silvertone."

"And the rest of the traditions," Jessica adds.

"Mom and Dad's friend, Marco Carrasco, coming to the house dressed like Santa Claus and stealing presents from under our tree."

"Your old crony Allen making sugar-covered walnuts."

"Which always seemed to have a shell or two left intact because he'd had a few too many Buds while making them."

"Singing Christmas Carols in our neighborhood."

"We were pretty good. Not von Trapp family good, but not bad."

Michael sings, "*Raindrops on roses and whiskers on kittens.*" His baritone is surprisingly good.

"We're more alike than different," Jessica comments.

"I always knew that," Michael replies.

"When you started coming home from college, you'd stay up all night."

"Squinting at the colored Christmas lights – "

"I still do that."

"And watching old Christmas movies on KCRA until I nodded out. I inevitably woke up around midnight to the Vatican's Christmas Eve mass."

"You see, it's not as bad as you think it is."

"Just let me make it through December."

Chapter 15

The fog drifts outside the window of Jessica's house. Inside, Jessica and Brandon watch a VHS copy of *A Christmas Carol*. She sits on the couch. He sits in a chair nearby, scanning his phone.

"Did I do something?" she asks.

"Sorry, what?"

"Are you upset with me?"

He gets to his feet.

"I think we should take a break," he replies.

"There is something wrong."

"You're too wrapped up in Christmas. I don't get it."

"It's once a year."

"Not for you."

"It makes me feel good."

"Not me," Brandon answers.

"That hurts."

"It's too much."

"That's not true."

"You're more interested in your family. And doing for others. Not me."

"I have room in my heart for all of it. For all of you."

"I wish that were true."

He tucks the phone in his pocket and leaves her

sitting alone on the couch, the blue light of the television flickering on her face.

As the door closes softly, she squeezes her eyes shut. Tears trickle down her cheeks.

The McHenry Museum is housed in the original McHenry Public Library building. The library was built in 1912 with money left by Oramil McHenry, scion of the wealthy mansion-builder and landowner, specifically for a library. When the library moved to a larger site in 1971, the city of Modesto and the McHenry Museum and Historical Society, previously known as the Stanislaus County Historical Society, reached an agreement to allow the museum to move into the renovated space, which it did in 1972.

Michael often told Jessica about the many hours he and Allen spent in the library using the *Readers' Guide to Periodical Literature* while researching information for a school paper. The heavy, green-bound volumes were a Mother Lode of information for the inquiring mind. The library also housed a children's reading room in the basement, which her older brothers had used frequently growing up.

Jessica and Melissa wander through the McHenry Museum's display of Christmas artifacts. They idle in the lobby, gazing up at the massive artificial Christmas tree that fills the entry rotunda.

"Just like that?" Melissa asks.

"Just like that," Jessica answers.

"No explanation?"

"Not enough."

"Men."

"It's probably okay. I was thinking the same thing."

"You both seemed to be doing so well."

"It was a battle. He doesn't get it."

"Get what."

"Why I love Christmas so much. Why it's important to me. Why it makes me feel good."

"That's definitely an irreconcilable difference."

"Why be with someone who doesn't feel the same way you do?"

"I never liked him, anyway."

"Me, neither."

They both laugh until they cry.

Jessica enjoyed visiting the museum and its collection of historical artifacts, photographs, and stories about Modesto and the Central Valley. The museum also hosted a number of community events, such as Poets' Corner and historical presentations, which Jessica often attended. She especially enjoyed the permanent exhibits dedicated to baseball and hometown boy George Lucas' film, *American Graffiti*. The bookstore stocked all her books and she liked browsing its collection of books by other local authors.

There was something about the museum that gave her a sense of place.

A familiar and comforting sight each year are the lights strung on top of Seely Tower, which simulate an abstract Christmas tree. For years, the building was the tallest in town, until the Red Lion Hotel, later the DoubleTree, was built. From almost anywhere in downtown, you could see the bright lights and know that Christmas is here. It reminded Jessica of Modesto from a simpler time when Modesto was much smaller and everything you needed was located downtown, whether it was a grocery store, a restaurant, a clothes store, a movie theater, or a toy store. She wonders what it would be like to live in that kind of town, that kind of time.

Later that night, Jessica and Melissa sit side-by-side in the first row of the loge at the State Theatre. Christmas music plays. They're waiting for the start of the traditional Christmas show by Dave Koz and Friends, this year featuring Jonathan Butler, Melissa Manchester, Michael Lington, and Chris Walker. Jessica is costumed as Marjorie Reynolds' character Linda Mason in the recreated Christmas movie scene of *Holiday Inn*. Melissa is dressed as Carol Kane's whimsically brutal Ghost of Christmas Present in *Scrooged*.

"I'm not in the spirit yet," Melissa says.

"You say that every year," Jessica replies.

"I play Christmas music earlier every year. Decorate earlier. Bake, watch movies, shop. All those things on my Christmas have-to-do-to-get-in-the-spirit list. Like you."

"Trying to recreate and hold onto that feeling is hard."

"If I start too soon, I'm burned out by the time it gets here. The excitement about Christmas turns into exhaustion. Like those kids with sugarplums dancing in their heads, I can't wait for it to be here and then, like Mom and Dad, I can't wait for it to be over and for school to start again. It's tiring."

"I never get to that point. I never panic. I know it will come when it's just right."

"That's because you're in the mood all the time."

"I don't care what time of year it is. It could be July or October. If I'm in a bad mood or depressed, I'll pop in a Christmas movie or play Christmas music, and all will be well."

"What do you want for Christmas this year?" Melissa asks.

"Besides peace on earth?"

"Yes, something more realistic. Something I can find on Amazon."

"If anyone has it, they do."

"They have everything else."

"It is attainable."

"Amazon ruling the world?"

"No, peace."

"Some day."

"I can only hope."

"You, at least, are doing something every day to make your Christmas wish come true."

"Seriously, I think as you grow older, your Christmas list gets smaller and the things you really want for the holidays can't be bought."

"You're going to be a cheap Christmas date."

"Doing for others. That's all the gift I need."

"That'll put you at the top of Santa's nice list."

"It's so simple and doable. Any time you feel down, do something for someone. It's the best therapy ever."

"I want to be you when I grow up."

"Be careful what you wish for."

The Bedford Falls Shop is crammed with shoppers searching for that special gift; the gift nobody else will have thought of.

Jessica is alone. She's working the cash register. She can barely keep up with the sales, questions, and other distractions.

Closing time arrives. An exhausted Jessica shuts everything down for the night.

"No, no, no!" she says.

The display case that held the silver bell ornament is empty.

Michael's house overflows with the Rivers family, as they gather for their annual December birthday celebration/family Christmas gift exchange. It's early this year because of holiday commitments and travel schedules.

In the kitchen, Melissa and her boyfriend, thirty-five-year old Gary, graze on the munchies spread across the countertops.

In the great room, holiday music plays in the background. A muted college football game runs on the TV.

Pictures of Jessica's parents, Daniel Rivers, Sr. and Cora Rivers, and their middle child, John, are displayed in a prominent place on the fireplace mantle.

Dan, Jr. sits on the couch with Linda. They munch on appetizers and watch the game. Jared and Travis play grab-ass on the floor in front of them.

In the massive entryway to the house, Michael and Jessica talk quietly and urgently.

"Couldn't we at least broach the idea?" she asks. "Maybe next Christmas they'd be open to donating instead of gifting?"

"Maybe they like the way things are."

"Maybe they'll like the new way better."

"Here you go again."

"Here I go again, what?"

"Orchestrating things."

"I think it's something we should consider. That's all I'm asking."

Michael glares at his sister. He takes a deep breath and plunges forward. "Why do you waste your time doing this stuff?" he asks.

"What 'stuff'?"

"Feeding the homeless. Planning the name draw. Entertaining old people. All this Christmas stuff."

"It's not a waste of time. It makes me happy. It makes other people happy."

"Why don't you do something important? Something that makes a difference?"

"I feel that, in a small way, I am. I'm doing something good. I can't do anything else."

"We both know you can."

"It's what I do. People count on me. Like we count on you."

"Jessica. Nobody cares."

Jessica reacts as if she's been slapped in the face.

Jessica and Melissa huddle in the hallway.

"Did you look everywhere?" Melissa asks.

"Everywhere. Inside and out," Jessica answers. "I couldn't find it anywhere."

"Find what?" Dan, Jr. asks as he passes to get to the bathroom.

"Someone stole her silver bell. The one from the movie."

"That's worth some money," he says.

"It's really not about the money," Jessica answers.

"Maybe it's in the hands of someone who needs it more, instead of being trapped in a display case," Melissa suggests. "Someone who needs Christmas now more than ever."

"I can only hope."

"Remember that young guy who was in the shop who needed a bath?" Melissa asks.

"Vaguely."

"He might have taken it. He seemed awfully interested. He certainly could use it."

"Maybe. I don't know. Everything's a jumble."

"I wouldn't tell Michael," Dan, Jr. suggests.

"I wasn't planning to. He would just imply I'm irresponsible."

"He wouldn't imply it, he'd say it," Dan, Jr. answers.

"He'd probably say it was for the best," Melissa continues. "That it's a sign from above that you should scale back on all the Christmas craziness."

"He wouldn't understand," Jessica replies. "He has nothing to hold onto in his life. He treats everything and everyone as expendable. If it doesn't benefit him, it's not important."

"That's a little harsh," Dan, Jr. says.

"I'm sorry. I'm not feeling very charitable right now."

"I'll help you look at the shop tomorrow," Melissa volunteers. "We'll leave no stone or shelf or elf unturned."

"I'll help you look around the house," Dan, Jr. adds.

"Thanks guys. I appreciate it."

The family sits on the sofa, chairs, and the floor, which is now strewn with shredded wrapping paper, torn ribbon, and discarded bows. Everyone is relaxed, food comatosed, and filled with Christmas spirit.

"This is a new Christmas song I've been working on," Jessica says.

Jessica slides a cassette into her small boom box, which she perched on a table. She hits play. A beautiful Christmas carol about home, family, and childhood fills the air. Everyone smiles.

Everyone but Michael. He gets up and crosses to the table. He hits the stop button.

Jessica can't believe what her big brother has done. She gathers her gifts. She grabs her coat and hat. She heads for the door.

Dan, Jr. intercepts her in the entryway.

"He can be an ass," he says.

"It's more than that."

"He's got a bunch going on."

"Good for him."

As she leaves, she sets the Christmas tree pin on a side table by the front door.

Chapter 16

The shop is closed. Jessica and Melissa sip tea and relax at the child-sized table in the children's corner.

"You'll find it," Melissa says. "When you least expect it."

"I'm counting on it."

"Positive thoughts."

"They're being crowded out by the negative ones."

"Doesn't it make you feel violated?"

"In a way, it does."

"I can't imagine getting robbed. Having some stranger poking around in my things."

"Now I know what it feels like."

"Seems like it's been one thing after another. First that, then Michael's smooth move at the family gathering."

"They say bad things come in threes. There may still be one more to come."

"He was out of line," Melissa says. " He doesn't get to do that, even if he is the big brother."

"Maybe he's right. Maybe it is time to grow up. Get over this 'obsession'."

"There's nothing wrong with you. He's got the problem. He's the one that hates Christmas."

"I wonder why. He used to love it."

"'AD'."

Jessica is confused.

"'After divorce,'" Melissa clarifies.

Jessica shrugs.

"He did apologize. He left a message later."

"Damage done."

"Michael got me thinking, though."

"About?"

"He said 'nostalgia' was a sickness."

"He can be such a butt."

"So, I did a bit of research," Jessica says.

"Typical. Such a deadtreehead. Any reason to haunt a musty old library."

"'Nostalgia' comes from the Greek word *nostos*, or homecoming. Homer came up with that in *The Odyssey*."

"Always the Greeks. Or the Romans. Or the Babylonians."

"It's more than the usual homesickness."

"Like being at summer camp?"

"It was a longing to feel at home in the world. Finally. On the surface, the story was about Ulysses' journey home. It involved trials and tribulations. Encounters with mythic creatures, sickness, love, and the dead."

"Just your usual bedtime story."

"The end of the journey is the discovery of who you truly are. An arriving at that place where you really belong."

"So, it's not really about Christmas."

"No, it's not," Jessica answers.

"Never has been," Melissa adds.

Jessica shakes her head, then passes a letter to Melissa.

"The building's been sold," she says.

"You're kidding me."

Melissa scans the document.

"Will you have to close?" she asks.

"Maybe."

"That would be horrible."

"Might be a sign."

"Might be number three."

The parking lot of Vintage Faire Mall is packed. Cars prowl looking for an empty space close to an entry.

Inside, people stream along the storefronts of both levels. Carolers sing. Clerks in kiosks entice. Children rush their parents from shop to shop. Teenagers on dates flirt, share a shake, and try not to show they're interested. Exhausted mothers and fathers rest in the overstuffed chairs. Older couples smile at the hubbub, recalling the days when they experienced all this.

Three volunteers wait behind the counter at the Soroptimist Christmas gift booth. Nearby, Jessica stands beside an artificial Christmas tree festooned with paper tags. Each has the name of a child whose family can't afford much for Christmas. And what they'd like Santa to bring them.

"I'd love to get them everything they want," a familiar male voice says.

Startled, Jessica turns to see Josh.

"Me, too," she says.

"You do this every year?" he asks.

"I do."

"Me, too. "

"I'm surprised we haven't bumped into each other before."

"I'm not. If you were here, I'd come back later."

"Was it that bad?" she asks.

"You broke my heart."

Jessica turns back to scan the tags.

"They all want bikes," she says.

"So, did I."

"There's nothing that says Christmas like a brand-new bike."

"Join me for a drink?" he asks.

"You sure?"

"Absolutely."

Jessica and Josh sit in a booth at a mall restaurant. She nurses a coffee. He a glass of red wine.

"He was always tough on you," Josh says.

"Expectations are lethal."

"That's what big brothers do."

"What if he's right?" Jessica asks.

"That's for you to find out."

"I guess I knew that."

"I don't deal much with the past or the future. For me, it's all about right now. This moment. The grapes keep me focused on the present."

A five-year-old boy races past them chased by his young mother.

For a moment, Jessica drifts away, distracted by a memory.

Josh notices.

"No amount of guilt can solve the past," he continues. "No amount of anxiety can change the future."

"You come up with that?"

"I wish. I read it somewhere."

"Ah, guilt and anxiety. Two of my closest friends."

"We learn from our past, but dwelling on it keeps us from being fully present to life in the moment. We can hope for the future, but it also keeps us from experiencing what's happening here and now."

"I have no regrets," Jessica says.

"That's good. Regret is pointless. It has no value. We learn from our mistakes and move on."

"There might be one regret."

"I'm sorry you lost your baby."

"Our baby."

"That was a horrible Christmas."

"I've seen a few."

Josh touches her on the sleeve.

"Where are you?" he asks.

"Back in high school."

Josh's reaction to this is mixed.

"Many times, you've said Christmas is a good time for looking back," he says.

"Not everyone feels that way."

"And for telling the truth."

"If you can't say it at Christmas, when can you?" Jessica says, quoting a line from *Love Actually*. She raises her cup. "To old times."

"To now."

Josh places his hand on Jessica's. She hesitates, then withdraws it.

"I'm sorry, but I've got to get back to the shop."

"Did I say something?"

"No. I need to find something."

"What did you lose?"

"My angel bell."

"Your what . . .?"

"The bell from *Wonderful Life*. It disappeared from the display case and I'm not sure where it is."

"That's too bad, Jess. I know how much it means to you."

"Means almost as much to me as it did to Clarence."

"It'll turn up."

"I could use a Christmas miracle about now."

Jessica leans against the railing, mid-span of Dry Creek Bridge. The swollen water roars below her. She looks upstream to where it's been, she gazes below at where it is, and sweeps her eyes downstream to where it's going. The past feeds into the present and then flows downstream, into the future and out of sight.

She recalls the words the limping boy said to her outside the church.

"When you look up river, then look at where you're standing, then look down river, it's as if the past, present, and future are streaming right before your eyes. You learn from yesterday, live for today, and hope for tomorrow."

Everything is connected, isn't it, she repeats to herself.

She closes her eyes and softly sings, "*I wish there was a river I could skate away on.*" Joni Mitchell's song swirls inside her head.

Jessica had never thought of "River" as a Christmas song until it was used in a holiday episode of another *thirtysomething*. It was used again in *Love Actually*. It had become one of her favorite Christmas songs and was one of Mitchell's most recorded compositions.

Back home Jessica thinks about how it was before

Michael soured on Christmas. He had once enjoyed
creating one-of-a-kind gifts for the family. Jessica recalls
one homemade present in particular that was especially
memorable. It is the one she is staring at now, which
sits on the top of her bedroom dresser. It is a handmade,
three-dimensional, glass-fronted shadow box. Inside
are objects that, for Michael, represent things uniquely
Jessica. He had done it for each sibling. Hers includes
a photo of the two of them at Picnic Day in UC Davis,
their dad's fudge recipe, sheet music, a tiny Christmas
book, a paint brush, and a small acrylic heart. Gazing at
each object, she realizes how much she misses the old
version of her brother.

Jessica and Dan, Jr. concentrate on a thousand piece
puzzle featuring six snowmen against a background of
snow. An audio recording of *A Christmas Carol* plays in
the background.

*"Are you the Spirit, sir, whose coming was foretold
to me?" asked Scrooge.*

"I am!"

*The voice was soft and gentle. Singularly low, as
if instead of being so close beside him, it were at a
distance.*

"Who, and what are you?" Scrooge demanded.

"I am the Ghost of Christmas Past."

"Long Past?" inquired Scrooge: observant of its dwarfish stature.

"No. Your past."

"Could you have picked anything more difficult?" Dan, Jr. asks rhetorically.

"It's not all that bad."

"They all look the same. Six white bodies, six top hats, six red scarves, twelve coal eyes, six carrot noses, twelve tree branch arms, and six pairs of black rubber boots. I'm surprised the 'partridge in a pear tree is missing.'"

"A piece at a time, a piece at a time, grasshopper."

"I understand that from a metaphysical point of view, but not a practical one. My head hurts."

"Your feet stink and you don't love Jesus."

"Careful now," Dan, Jr., replies, smiling. "This isn't the time of year to be taking the Lord's name in vain."

"It's not in vain. It's in jest."

"Nonetheless, I'd do a few Hail Marys."

Jessica jumps to her feet and mimes throwing a long bomb. She's a bit of a jock, too.

"I don't want to be anywhere near you when the lightning bolt strikes."

Jessica sits and slips another puzzle piece in place.

"Working on a puzzle is like writing a book or driving a car," she says. "Keep your eyes on the page, or the road, directly in front of you."

Scrooge reverently disclaimed all intention to offend

*or any knowledge of having wilfully "bonneted" the
Spirit at any period of his life. He then made bold to
inquire what business brought him there.*

"Your welfare!" said the Ghost.

*Scrooge expressed himself much obliged, but could
not help thinking that a night of unbroken rest would
have been more conducive to that end. The Spirit must
have heard him thinking, for it said immediately:*

"Your reclamation, then. Take heed!"

*It put out its strong hand as it spoke, and clasped
him gently by the arm.*

"Rise, and walk with me!"

"I'm sorry we couldn't find the bell," Dan, Jr. says.

"It was a long shot. I hardly ever bring it home.
There was no rhyme or reason for it being here."

"Not to worry. It'll show up."

"I'm curious what else is on your mind to bring
you here on this chilly day," Jessica wonders. "Not my
reclamation, I hope."

"No, the first one."

"Ah, my welfare, then."

"Yes. I thought I'd check in."

"No need, big brother. I'm doing fine."

"You shouldn't be so hard on yourself."

"Am I?"

"I think so."

"'Tis the season."

"You give so much of yourself. Maybe too much."

"I'm doing it for others, not for myself. If it was only for myself, it's not really giving to others, is it?"

"It takes strength to accept that we have limitations. That we can only do so much."

"I understand that. Sometimes I get too wrapped up in all of it. But, I usually figure it out."

"Not always."

"I disagree."

"I'm reminded of something from the *Tao Te Ching* by Lao Tzu and his philosophy about flexibility. *Yield and overcome; Bend and be straight; Empty and be full; Wear out and be new; Have little and gain; Have much and be confused.* I think it means if you are truly whole, if you are receptive, all good things will come to you."

"I wasn't prepared for a lesson in Taoism."

"Isn't that what Christmas is all about though. The hope that, in the end, our better natures will prevail? That if we open our hearts and are receptive, we will be filled with the Christmas spirit?"

"It is. The season notwithstanding. It's just more intense this time of year."

"Here's another lesson from Chairman Lao. *Water is fluid, soft, and yielding. But water will wear away rock, which is rigid and cannot yield. As a rule, whatever is fluid, soft, and yielding will overcome whatever is rigid and hard. This is another paradox: what is soft is strong.*"

"Am I the water or the rock?"

"Depends on the day."

Chapter 17

Early the next morning, Jessica washes and dries her coffee cup, then places it in the cupboard. She reaches for her Advent Calendar. She opens the flap labeled with the number "1." It reveals an image of Marley's Ghost from the movie, *A Christmas Carol*. Her eyes stare blankly. Her movements seem dream-like, as if under a spell.

Jessica trudges outside to retrieve the morning newspaper from the driveway. Returning, she reaches for the handle of the front door. She notices something out of the ordinary about the knocker. There appears to be a face etched into the metal. The face of her father. Mildly stunned, she blinks her eyes and peers closer. Whatever was there is gone.

That night, Jessica tastes a deliciously decorated sugar cookie shaped like a bell. She seems transported. Like Proust's *madeleine* moment, that taste of cookie conjures up a memory of a day she experienced as a young child making fudge with her father. She sees them pour the gooey chocolate into a chipped oval platter, her father dabbing a smidge of fudge on her nose, and her biting into the finished fudge and smacking her lips.

Her sugar cookie reminds Jessica of the many

luscious tastes of Christmas.

Jessica savors a figgy pudding during "Breakfast with Santa" at the Gallo Center for the Arts. All around her, friends and neighbors chatter and linger over the bounty.

Jessica carefully decorates a gingerbread house at the local Boys & Girls Club. The children shout and laugh, as they devour the building materials.

Jessica sips tea at the benefit for the Center for Human Services held in the banquet room adjoining Green's Restaurant. Volunteers mingle, as they pour the soothing beverage for donors and guests.

Jessica devours a butter slathered sticky bun at Village Baking Company. The bakery is full with families feasting on the freshly baked tastes of the season or buying them to share with family and friends.

Jessica distributes red plastic Christmas stockings filled with assorted hard candies at the Senior Center. The elder residents seem enchanted by memories of their childhood, as they eat the merry fare.

Jessica attends a neighbor's holiday party. There is food, friends, and music. The mood is joyous, as everyone crowds around tables filled with seasonal edibles.

Jessica hands out fruit to the homeless. Their skeletal eyes are filled with gratitude more dear than gold.

Jessica eats steaming chestnuts on the street outside Macy's in San Francisco. Other San Franciscans crowd around the small cart, seemingly taken back to a gentler time.

Jessica trades cookies with friends at a cookie exchange hosted by Melissa and Gary. Everyone seems to have abandoned the holiday hustle and bustle, as they dip their cookies in hot chocolate.

Late one night, Jessica sits alone in the kitchen, sipping eggnog and eating a slice of fruit cake. Bewitched by a memory.

A grandfather clock chimes the midnight hour.

"Bet it doesn't taste as good as my fudge," a gentle male voice says.

Jessica reacts to the paternal voice. She's not shocked. It's almost as if she were expecting his visit.

"I've never tasted anything as yummy as your fudge, Daddy."

Daniel Rivers, Sr., as he looked at age sixty, stands in the kitchen doorway. Translucent and glowing.

"You seem lonely," he says.

"I'm not really."

"Even when you're in a crowd, you seem so alone."

"We're all alone together."

"'Loneliness is absolute.'"

Jessica reacts to her own words.

"It's easier," she replies.

"Why are you beating yourself up, sweet pea?"

"I expect too much."

"'Expectations are lethal.'"

She's sorry now she said that, too.

"When things don't turn out, I get disappointed. Then mad. Then I give up. And don't care anymore. And don't want anyone around."

"You're not that kind of person."

"Feels like it lately."

"You were the one who gave people the benefit of the doubt," her father adds.

"Taking the high road isn't always the best road. It's not always appreciated."

"Your compassion is what makes you … you."

"Everyone wants me to change. To be something I'm not."

"You're fine the way you are. Just be yourself."

"If I could change, maybe a tad, I could make some people happy."

"Things around you, outside things, will change. You can't stop that. Embrace it. But, as for you, there's just one you. Embrace that, too."

"I feel like I've missed something. That maybe I didn't do something I should have."

"Don't lament what you may have missed. What you didn't do. Celebrate what you experienced. What you did do."

"Thanks."

"For what?"

"For always knowing what to say. For being there. For being the rock. For being someone we could always count on. For sacrificing so much for us kids."

"I would do anything for you kids."

"You make me feel that everything will be all right."

"It could be, if … "

"If what?"

"If people could only learn to treat each other better. To love, honor, and respect each other. To simply take care of each other."

The clock chimes again.

Her father disappears.

Jessica takes another sip of nog and another bite of cake.

Chapter 18

Jessica opens the flap labeled with the number "5" on her Advent Calendar. It reveals an image of Dudley the angel from the movie, *The Bishop's Wife*.

That night, Jessica lingers by the Christmas tree in her living room. She touches the boughs. She appears lost in another world.

The silken needles of her tree recall the heartwarming touches of the holidays.

Jessica gently strokes the lighted and glitter-covered Christmas scene fabric artwork in the Mulberry Lane shop. She watches as nearby shoppers act like children, as they touch ornaments and nutcrackers.

Jessica sits at a wooden table inside the Barnes & Noble bookstore. She is surrounded by copies of her children's Christmas books. She feels the cloth cover of one book before opening and inscribing it. She hands it to an excited young girl of about eight, who clutches the book to her heart.

Jessica runs her hand along the bare adobe wall of the Custom House in the plaza of Old Monterey, which has been decorated for Christmas. She enters to see re-enactors in *Californio* costume dancing the *fandango*.

Jessica caresses the wooden baby Jesus in the center of the nativity collection in her home. Whatever burden she may be carrying seems lightened.

Jessica compacts the round face of a snowman made of freshly fallen snow at the snowline above Twain Harte. She watches as other visitors exuberantly pelt one another with snowballs.

Jessica rubs her thumb over the soft stenciling of the '50s-era ornament dangling from the decorated Christmas tree in the lobby of the DoubleTree Hotel.

Jessica walks the banks of iced-over Pine Crest Lake. She tilts back her head and swallows a falling snowflake. She observes children lying on their backs, arms and bare hands outstretched, creating snow angels.

Jessica fluffs the tufts of cotton surrounding the miniature scene of Bedford Falls in her shop. As she studies the tiny figurines of Mary and George Bailey, she's trapped in a troubling thought.

Jessica spreads the velvety leaves of a poinsettia plant tucked among rows and rows of plants in the Duarte Nursery greenhouse. The other shoppers seem carried away by nature's gentle, comforting touch.

In her living room a few nights later, Jessica slides her fingertips down the Christmas stocking hanging from her fireplace mantle. It is the richly embroidered southwest one with the crazy cactus and coyote.

Her Christmas clock announces the late hour by playing "Joy to the World."

"Your father and I spent many hours on that," a reassuring female voice says.

"It's beautiful, Mommy."

Cora Rivers, frozen in time at fifty-nine, stands near the fireplace.

"Like you," she says.

"I bet you say that to all your kids."

"I confess I do."

"We forgive you."

"That's so you."

"What?" Jessica asks.

"So charitable."

"Isn't 'charitable' another word for 'co-dependent'?"

"Depends on the circumstance."

"Doesn't everything?"

"It's tempered by your love. I've never known anyone so full of love as you," her mother adds.

"Again, a problem."

"Too bad the rest of the world isn't as compassionate and accepting as you."

"That's a heavy burden to carry. I recall one man died because of it."

"Let there be peace on earth, my child, and let it begin with you."

"Are you happy where you are?"

"I'm with your father. But, I miss this time of year."

"Christmas isn't the same without you."

"Even though I spoiled you with too many gifts?"

"We were spoiled. But it was part of what made Christmas Christmas. I love Christmas so much because of you."

"I did it for you. For all of you. I loved sharing all of it with my babies."

"Now we share it. Thanks to you."

"I wish I could be there with you. I miss you."

"We miss you, too."

"It was lonely once you'd all grown up and started your own lives."

"You had Dad. And the kitties."

"But I didn't have you kids. When Johnny finally moved out, that was it. You were all gone. Do you know how lonely that was?"

Staring into her mother's sad face, Jessica thinks, *It really is a lonely world. A writer once commented that it was not possible for two people to truly know each other. No matter how close the husband and wife, the father and son, the lover and beloved, parents and children, we are all locked inside ourselves, which says something horrible about our lack of knowledge; about our hopeless and terrible and sadly permanent loneliness. And something about the loneliness of the individual trying to find meaning in their isolation. The doctor said my Mom died of heart failure. But she really died from the absoluteness of loneliness.*

"I wish we had paid more attention," Jessica says.

"It wouldn't have changed anything."

"I don't want to believe that."

"You don't have that kind of power."

"We should have been able to do something."

"It was too late."

The Christmas clock plays "Mary, Did You Know?."

Her mother disappears.

Jessica touches the embroidered stocking.

Chapter 19

Jessica opens the flap labeled with the number "10" on her Advent Calendar. It reveals an image of Bing Crosby, Danny Kaye, Rosemary Clooney, and Vera-Ellen from the movie, *White Christmas*.

Sitting in the sun porch that night, Jessica winds up a musical matchbox. The sound of "White Christmas" fills the room. She's entranced.

Her most adored Christmas song heralds the jubilant sounds of the Yuletide.

Jessica bounces up and down to the cacophony of Modesto's Celebration of Lights Christmas parade, as it winds through downtown. Thumping marching and rock bands, rumbling street rods, squealing children, tooting trucks, and jingling jingle bells fill the night air.

Jessica attends CarolFest at California State University, Stanislaus. The attendees are enraptured by the sacred songs.

Jessica sings the Messiah at the First Methodist Church. The voices of her fellow choir members, the congregants, and guests rise to the heavens.

Jessica sways in her seat, as she watches *The Nutcracker* performed by Central West Ballet at the

Gallo Center. The audience appears spirited to the Land of Sweets.

Jessica follows a group of carolers serenading shoppers at the Dickens Faire in front of the McHenry Mansion. As they listen, the adults become as bewitched as their children.

Jessica is transfixed on Christmas Tree Lane by a display of Christmas lights synced to rock music. The sidewalks are filled with observers, many of whom dance to the music.

Jessica pops a cassette of *A Happy Trails Christmas* by Roy Rogers and Dale Evans into her Walkman and rides her bike through the college neighborhood. She merrily hums along with the songs.

Jessica sits in a pew at St. Stanislaus Church listening to the Modesto Symphony and Choir perform their Candlelight Concert. The sanctuary is filled to the brim with celebrants, who share the holy spirit of the music.

Jessica dances as a rockabilly band belts out holiday songs beneath a giant flashing Christmas tree at Tenth Street Plaza during *ModestoView*'s Rockin' Holiday. Man-made snow floats through the night sky and onto the bystanders, who clap along with the tunes.

In her sun porch on another night, Jessica plays and sings the same Christmas song Michael abruptly turned off at the family gathering.

A vintage Charlie Brown clock plays the theme from "A Charlie Brown Christmas" by Vince Guaraldi to mark the fading hour.

"Music is the universal language of love, peace, and understanding," another very recognizable male voice says. "It can transfigure us. Music is life. That's why our hearts have beats."

"Sweet Johnny. You knew that well. And lived it. Before we lost you."

John Rivers, her youngest older brother, stands silhouetted by the sun porch windows.

"You're gifted, you know," he says.

"That's high praise considering the source."

"I wish you'd let it go."

"What?"

"The fear of failing. I don't want you to regret not doing what you wanted – needed – to do. Like I did. Like Michael did. He wanted to be a triple threat like you. A writer, a musician, an artist."

"It's hard."

"Don't I know it. I had my shot. Problem is, I liked home cooking," her brother adds.

"So, do I. Plus, you could never say 'no'."

"None of us could."

"It can be a problem."

"Don't give up hope. Without hope and dreams, we've got nothing."

"I still have most of your guitars."

"I know. I'm glad they found a good home."

"I try not to play too many dirges. I know you didn't like them."

"I liked to rock. It's not church."

"I wish we could have played together."

"Me, too."

"I thought it would be harder. It's hard, don't get me wrong, But, once I got over worrying about it and stressing about being as good as you, I discovered it wasn't as tough as I thought it would be."

"It never is."

"Then when I started playing with people and got in the groove, it felt so right."

"That's the power of music."

"And love. And family."

The clock plays another song from "A Charlie Brown Christmas."

Her brother disappears.

Jessica plays and sings her original Christmas song from the top.

Chapter 20

Jessica opens the flap labeled with the number "15" on her Advent Calendar. It reveals an image of Edmund Gwen playing Santa Claus from the movie, *Miracle on 34th Street*.

In her bedroom that night, Jessica smells the peppermint candle guttering on the side table beside her reading chair. She's trapped in a reverie.

Her candle summons the delightful smells associated with this time of the year.

Jessica inhales the holiday aromas wafting through the air at the yearly gathering of faculty, staff, alumni, and friends of the Modesto Junior College Foundation at the McHenry Museum.

Jessica crinkles her nose at the salty ocean smells, as she watches the parade of Christmas-themed boats glide through Santa Cruz Harbor.

Jessica smiles as a whiff of sweet chocolate drifts under her nose inside the See's Candy Store. Young and old can't help but be intoxicated by the decadence.

Jessica sniffs the crisp cinnamon emanating from the candy canes dangling beneath the tree at Galletto Ristorante. A young girl presses her nose against a low hanging cane. Jessica is stilled by a memory.

Jessica breathes in the heavenly incense floating through the Napa caves hosting Carols in the Caves. Like her, the other revelers rejoice in the experience.

Jessica waves the steam of freshly-cooked turkey toward her nose, as she waits for dinner at Noah's Hof Brau. She observes other patrons savoring the seasonal scents.

Jessica draws in the fresh evergreen coming from the Christmas wreaths lining the walls of Hart Floral. A couple in their twenties quietly arguing while they walk suddenly stop, as they reach the corridor of wreaths and are enveloped in the bouquet.

Jessica searches for the source of the relaxing fragrance of vanilla and nutmeg, as she watches the final Beach Blanket Babylon Christmas Show in San Francisco. The odors send her back to some long-ago holiday kitchen.

Jessica steps through a curling puff of the burning candle, as she follows a docent dressed in nineteenth century clothes on the Candlelight Tour of the merrily decorated McHenry Mansion. The waxy smoke encircles her head like a garland.

A few nights later, Jessica snuffs in a noseful of smothering fog. It swirls around the gravestones in the cemetery beside Mission San Juan Bautista following the performance of *La Pastorela* by *El Teatro Campesino*.

The mission bell clangs the hour.

"Apartment hunting?" a teasing and long-lost voice asks.

"Very funny, Allen."

Allen Mullens, Michael's childhood pal, drapes an arm around a stone statue of an angel.

"Just trying to keep things light," he says.

"Almost as funny as your best friend."

"Your brother has no sense of humor."

"He used to."

"So, did you."

"Life does that."

"That's the easy way out."

"The best I can do right now."

"You've grown up."

"Life does that, too."

"I remember that scrawny little kid who had acne, wore her hair in a bun, and was ready anytime for a late dinner or early breakfast at Denny's."

"Usually when you and Michael had had too much to drink."

"You know, sometimes I don't think you guys understand where he's coming from."

"And where's that?"

"Oh, I don't know. Maybe love, concern, protectiveness. Watching over the nest."

"We've all found our wings. A long time ago."

"Doesn't change anything. He's been programmed to keep an eye out for all of you. Especially with your folks gone so young."

"We can watch out for ourselves. I keep telling him that."

"Don't be such a tough guy."

"I try not to be. Problem is, I don't think before I speak."

"You should definitely think before you speak. Or, is it sit before you spit?"

"Yogi's got nothing on you."

"Ah, Mr. Berra. My hero. But seriously, folks. He only wants what's best for all of you."

"His heart is in the right place."

"Always has been."

"I know."

"You always talk about taking the high road. Maybe you should try a little forgiveness," her brother's *compadre* adds.

"Thanks for the reminder, Otis."

"Just the messenger."

"One I wish was still here. We could use your unusual point of view. Your humor often put things in perspective."

"Humor's always in need of repair."

"Clever, Jimmy."

"Another hero."

"Parrotheads rule."

"Deadheads drool."

"Ever the jester," Jessica says.

"You staying the night or driving back?"

"Driving back."

"It's pretty foggy. Be careful."

"You sound like my big brother."

"Feel like it, too."

"You were. More than him, sometimes."

"I remember coming back from here one time with Michael. And our wives at the time. He had to open the car door to see the center divider."

"That's pretty foggy."

"Keep your eyes open."

"I will."

"Don't do what I wouldn't, or couldn't, do."

The mission bell clangs again.

Her brother's dearest friend disappears.

Back home that night and safely in bed, Jessica blows out the peppermint candle.

Chapter 21

Jessica opens the flap labeled with the number "20" on her Advent Calendar. It reveals an image of Clara and the Nutcracker from the ballet, *The Nutcracker*.

In the dining room later that night, Jessica sees, without seeing, the slowly turning light wheel, as it splashes colors across the aluminum Christmas tree. She appears to be in a hypnotic trance.

Her color wheel evokes the kaleidoscopic sights that help make the season shiny and bright.

Jessica marvels at the creativity of the Fantasy of Trees in the lobby of the Gallo Center. The holiday displays have been created by different designers to raise money for Community Hospice.

Jessica watches the excited faces of children of all ages lined up to sit on Santa's lap at the HGTV Christmas Pavilion. The frown she'd been wearing is turned upside down.

Jessica visits the Chartreuse Muse gallery on the third Thursday Art Walk. Her eyes brim with wonder at the talent and creativity of the local artists. The gallery goers appraise the arts and crafts.

Jessica rides her bike dressed as *Sinterklaas* among

a throng of other Santa Clauses riding sparklingly lit and decorated bikes through downtown. It's SantaCon. The joy radiates from everyone's eyes.

Jessica keeps her eyes on "The Grinch," as she and a pack of runners chase Dr. Seuss' Christmas character in the Spirit of Giving 5K Run and Walk, coursing through the streets of her neighborhood.

Jessica is dressed as Mary Bailey in the scene at the high school dance, as she watches *It's a Wonderful Life* on the big screen at the historic State Theatre in downtown. Other moviegoers are also dressed in characters from the film. The celluloid images gleam in their upturned eyes.

Jessica assembles a complicated puzzle featuring the traditional image of Santa Claus by Thomas Nast. Her merry eyes twinkle, as she fits the last piece.

Jessica holds a photo of her mother and father, Johnny and Allen, as part of the Light Up a Life Tree Lighting Ceremony in front of Memorial Medical Center to benefit Community Hospice. There is a sadness, but also a collective comfort, in the eyes of the onlookers.

Jessica follows close behind Joseph and Mary and other local townspeople through Salinas, as they re-enact the search for shelter at each *posada* (inn) in Bethlehem. Her reverent eyes weep with love for the homeless parents of Jesus.

As Christmas draws nigh, Jessica spends the evening cocooned on the couch in her living room watching old 8mm home movies projected onto a tattered screen. The images shine in her misty eyes.

A lonesome train whistle signals the late hour.

"Have you seen the like of me before?" a voice from the immediate past asks.

"I have seen your kind, Chris."

"We but turn another page," the voice continues.

"One shadow more?"

Christopher Walsh, Michael's college roommate at UC Davis, sits at the end of the couch.

The film continues to roll.

"There's a time and place for nostalgia," he says.

"In old home movies?"

"In the past."

"Your old roomie hasn't usually thought so."

"Your brother likes reeling in the years."

"Until he loses control," she says.

"I think he thinks 'in the moment' is a bad yoga pose."

"He's too occupied putting out fires."

"'Doing instead of being.' That's not a good thing."

Jessica grimaces, recalling Brandon's accusation.

"You were a notorious 'doer,'" she replies.

"Guilty as charged. Until I couldn't."

"It's hard to ignore the needs."

"It takes focus."

"Strike one."

"And courage."

"Strike two."

"And generosity."

"You're outta there!"

"Give yourself some credit."

"When it's due."

"You're one of the most generous people I've ever known," her brother's roommate adds. "This world could use more like you."

"For an irresponsible, judgmental, and co-dependent Luddite with a low self-image who lives alone in the past, while doing unimportant and unambitious things and who will never amount to anything and go anywhere."

"Whew. Take a breath, girl."

She does.

"I disagree. You're not a Luddite," he continues, smiling. "You know exactly where you're going. You simply need some help remembering how to get there."

If you don't know where you're going, you might not get there, springs to mind, as Jessica remembers the words spoken by the old woman with the flute.

The train whistle blows once more.

Her brother's college comrade disappears.

Jessica watches the double-exposed film, as a whale jumps through an aluminum Christmas tree.

With Chris' words echoing in her ears, Jessica steps outside. She eyes the *luminarias* lighting the path to her front door. They have been blown over by the wind.

All but five.

It's the final week of shopping. The last of the procrastinators rush around downtown searching for the perfect gift, or at least what's left to get when everything to get has already been gotten.

Josh sits in a child-sized chair at the child-sized table in Jessica's shop paging through her children's Christmas books.

"The bad penny returns," Jessica says.

Josh looks up, pleasantly startled by her sudden appearance.

"Sorry?"

"As in, 'a bad penny always turns up.'"

Josh struggles to get out of the chair. He resembles Bishop Brougham trying to extricate himself from the newly varnished and sticky chair in *The Bishop's Wife*.

Jessica lends a hand.

"I hope you don't see me that way."

"I don't."

"I'm glad."

"Last minute shopping?" she asks.

"These were so wonderful I wanted to get more for my nieces and nephews."

"I'm happy you like them."

"They're so you."

"Where's Savannah?"

"At a movie. She's not a big shopper."

They stare at each other for a long moment.

Jessica breaks the spell. "Let's get you checked out."

"Sorry?"

"The books. Let's ring them up."

Melissa is behind the register. She looks exhausted.

"Well, what a pleasant surprise," she says, as Josh reaches the head of the line.

"Hello, Melissa. It's been a while."

"Too long. You know, if it were up to me, we would have kept you instead of her," she tilts her head toward her sister.

"I've got to run to the post office," Jessica cuts in. "Would you like to walk with me?"

"I think I can manage that," Josh answers.

"Be careful," Melissa says. "You know how she gets this time of year."

"I do," he replies. "I miss it."

Outside the store, they linger a moment in front of the display window.

"Did you see anything you want?" Jessica asks.

"Sorry?"

"For Savannah. Is there anything Savannah might

want? Everything is deeply discounted."

"No, she's not into movies or holidays."

"That's a shame since you are."

Josh reacts to this reality.

"She's often said mementos are nothing but dust catchers," he replies.

"How sentimental."

"She can be."

"Well then, we're off to Santa's temporary seasonal office."

Jessica moves down the street, followed closely by Josh. They pass holiday-themed windows and harried shoppers.

"We had some good Christmases," he says.

"We did."

They turn into a wide alleyway to get to the post office. On either side are trash cans and bins waiting for pickup. Josh stops and lifts the lid on one.

"What are you doing?" Jessica asks. "Are things that bad?"

"You never know what you might find. Maybe a treasure. Something special someone didn't need anymore. There's no telling."

"Yuck. You don't really do that, do you?"

"Sure. Easy way to avoid spending money on Christmas gifts," he smiles. "Just call me Mr. Jonas."

"Sorry?" It's her turn to be confused.

"The junk man from Ray Bradbury's novel,

Dandelion Wine. He collected and shared what everyone else thought was junk. He only asked that people take something they truly wanted, something they would use and treasure, and leave something of their own in exchange."

He lifts the lid on another container and peers inside.

"I'm going to leave you to your 'hobby'," Jessica says. "I have to get to the post office before Santa flies away."

"Good to see you, Jess."

"You, too," she says and walks away.

Josh starts to close the top on the trash container. He hears a faint tinkle. He stops. He lifts the lid again. Something catches his eye. He digs a little deeper. He pulls something from the debris. He turns to watch Jessica's retreating back and smiles.

Chapter 22

Jessica opens the flap labeled with the number "24" on her Advent Calendar. It reveals an image of George Bailey and Clarence the Angel from the movie, *It's a Wonderful Life*.

Jessica moves through her house not unlike the disembodied spirits who have visited.

In the kitchen, the eggnog coagulates.

In the living room, the needles on the Christmas tree drop to the floor.

In the sun porch, the musical matchbox slowly winds down and grinds to a halt.

In her bedroom, the peppermint candle wax hardens.

In the dining room, the color wheel is dark.

Jessica removes the Christmas cards from the mantle and puts them in the recycling bin.

She pours the glass of milk into the sink and tosses the small dish of peanut butter chocolate chip cookies, along with the note to Santa, into the trash.

She dumps the nativities into the wrong boxes.

She shoves the collection of decorative Santas unprotected into their storage containers.

She folds the stockings and tucks them into plastic bags.

The phone rings. She answers.

The shock on her face says it's not good.

Michael lies in a hospital bed at City Hospital. Battered and bruised and tethered to monitors and IVs.

"The tree won," he says.

"Were you drunk?"

"I'd had a few."

"You know better."

"I got lost. For a moment."

"Don't do it again."

"You, either. It's not worth it. I warned you. Don't be me. There's so much to live for."

Michael's doctor enters the room. He appears troubled.

"Let's allow him to rest, shall we?" he says.

"Can the others come in? All our family is here."

"I'd rather they didn't. Not now," he replies, his expression indicating it's much more serious than Jessica thought.

"Please. We won't stay long," she pleads, realizing what the look on his face might mean.

"Keep it short."

"We will, we will."

All the siblings but one stand in silence around

Michael's bed. Jessica notices they're arranged in birth order. Counterclockwise, oldest to youngest. The way they often did. Michael, Dan, Jr., an empty spot at the end of the bed where Johnny would have stood, Melissa, then Jessica.

Funny, she thinks, *we almost always stand in this order when we're together.*

She recollects a photograph of the family taken during some long-forgotten Valentine's Day. She can't recall if it was for *The Modesto Bee* or the telephone company newsletter. Mom and Dad stood in front of their five children.

We stood in birth order, facing our parents, each holding a hand-made paper valentine.

That photo made her think of one of the family's Disneyland trips. They were walking along the beach somewhere. Her mom stooped to pick up an abandoned, rusted toy automobile. She started to cry. "What's wrong?" Jessica had asked her. "Nothing," she replied, then hugged Jessica until she couldn't breathe.

As Jessica walks from the hospital, it dawns on her that Michael is the last link to the family's immediate history. When he's gone, it's gone. He will take their collective memory with him. With Mom and Dad both departed, as the eldest, he is the keeper of that history. He is the only one who remembers what has happened in their lives. Each event, every miniscule detail. When he is no longer around, if any of the family wants to know about anything that has ever happened, especially when they were young, there won't be anyone to ask about those moments. Michael knows the memories by heart. When he's not there, those memories won't be there, either. The rest of the family will be left to reconstruct them as best they can.

Scared and worried about her brother's condition, Jessica turns to the spirituality she had spoken with Melissa about. Not taking any chances on which God or entity will listen, she visits each of the city's houses of worship.

Jessica lights a candle for Michael at St. Stanislaus Church.

She bows her head in prayer at CrossPoint Church.

She listens to the rabbi at Congregation Beth Shalom.

She prays, head covered, at the Islamic Center.

She meditates at the Buddhist temple.

She sings along with the choir at Saint James African Methodist Episcopal Church.

She attends the late Christmas Eve service at First Methodist Church. She sits alone in the balcony pew. Forcing a smile, she acknowledges her fellow choir members and congregants.

Far to her right, she notices a solitary man.
He resembles Dudley from *The Bishop's Wife*.
He smiles at her.

Chapter 23

Jessica waits in the center of Dry Creek bridge. She peers into the raging waters below.

"It's the easy way out, you know," a sweet, drawling voice says. "A bit selfish, too,"

An amiable looking young man stands at the end of the bridge. He's almost transparent. At his back, what appears to be a small pair of wings rustles in the breeze.

"I'm good," Jessica answers.

"The last time I was in a place like this, I wasn't," he says.

"I'm not you."

"Then you've come to your senses?"

"Jury's still out."

He moves closer. A bright light seems to follow him.

"The name's George," he says, extending his hand.

"I know who you are."

"Can you even begin to imagine the wonderful things that won't happen without you?" George asks.

"Must not be that important if they're counting on me."

"Ah, but you have so much to offer. So much to give."

"If only."

"You have value. You have an important role to play in this community. And for the people who live here."

"I don't see it."

"Let people in. Embrace change. Be, don't do. Live here, now."

"It's too much."

"True happiness is living in the present. With people who value you. And your uniqueness."

"Could count them on one hand. Maybe."

"People you don't have to hold your breath around."

"Easier said than done."

"In order to have what you want, what you need, you must first be who you really are, then do what you have to do. Need to do. Find peace and everything will fall into place."

"Tone of voice. You're pontificating."

"I do that occasionally. From my days as an actor. I played a pilot once, you see. But, that's another story for another time."

"What are you now?"

He flaps his wings.

Jessica steps nearer to the railing of the bridge.

George moves closer.

"If you're happy with yourself, everyone and everything around you will be happy, too," he continues. "If you're grateful and thankful for who you are and what you have, happiness will always be there."

"I wish I could believe you."

"I feel sorry for those who don't understand that. It's a gift. You have it, young lady. You have it. All you have to do is accept it, enjoy it, and share it."

"That's too much responsibility."

"Over the years, I've found that true happiness isn't about getting what you want, but wanting what you've got."

"If only I knew what that was."

"I think you do."

George hands her the Christmas tree pin her brother gave her.

"Lecture over," he says.

The river rushes into the night.

Jessica stares at the joyfully decorated Arts and Crafts bungalow near downtown. She can't seem to make up her mind. Finally, she hurries up to the front door and knocks.

Josh answers. He is surprised, but pleasantly so. He steps aside.

Josh and Jessica sit facing each other on the couch in the cozy, cluttered living room. Their empty mugs sit on the coffee table.

"How can it possibly be your fault?" he asks.

"I don't know. It feels like it is."

"It was an accident."

"I hope so."

"What are you saying?"

"He made a mistake."

"You're making one now."

"By being here?"

"No, by believing you're to blame. I'm glad you're here."

"You are?"

"Absolutely."

"What about Savannah?"

"She's great, but – what about Brandon?"

"He's terrific, too. But, – "

"So, we both automatically assumed the other person loved someone else."

"You know what they say about assumptions."

Josh kisses her. Jessica kisses him back.

She opens her eyes, as if she's awakened from a spell. She kisses him again.

"Wow, I almost forgot," he says.

"You really don't love me?"

"Funny. Don't move."

He goes to the Christmas tree, selects a small wrapped box nestled beneath it, returns, and hands it to Jessica.

"You shouldn't have. I didn't get you anything," she says.

"Just open it."

Jessica unwraps the box and lifts the lid. She removes the tiny silver bell ornament stolen from the store.

"Where? When?"

"Remember that day I went 'dumpster diving'?"

"How can I forget that odd hobby."

"That's where and when."

"A treasure somebody didn't need anymore."

"You do."

"Thank you, Mr. Jonas."

Jessica smiles and kisses him again.

The bell tinkles.

Chapter 24

Michael rests comfortably in his hospital room. He appears much better. His color is back. He smiles at Jessica.

"Nothing ruptured, just bruised," he explains.

"You're a tough old bird," she replies.

"I'm trying to talk them into letting me out for Christmas."

"You can be very persuasive."

"When it's important enough."

He kisses his sister on the cheek. He notices the Christmas tree pin. He touches it.

"See you *mañana*, I hope," she says.

"You mean today. It's past midnight. Happy – uh, I mean, Merry Christmas, Jess."

"Merry Christmas, Michael."

As Jessica exits the hospital, it begins to snow. A rare occurrence for California's Central Valley. Jessica opens her mouth wide and gulps down the snowflakes.

Jessica trudges through the dark downtown. The song playing in her head is not a holiday song. It is one that often spun around in her brain.

There are places I'll remember
All my life, though some have changed
Some forever, not for better
Some have gone and some remain
All these places have their moments
With lovers and friends I still can recall
Some are dead and some are living
In my life, I've loved them all.

She is reminded that every day she encounters people and places, sights and sounds, memories and mementos that are, or symbolize, the then, now, and yet to be of her life. It is a chronicle of the immediate past, present, and future.

As Jessica moves past the Southern Pacific train depot, before turning to walk north along J Street, passing the buildings that once housed Toppers Jewelers, the Hotel Covell, J.C. Penney, Valley Sporting Goods, Sutton's Shoes, The Camera Center, Records, and Whites for Boys she reflects on where she's been and where she is now.

At each stage of life, we journey down roads that are familiar and well-traveled, having driven them our entire life. They are the roads taken. The landmarks we pass are beloved and well-known. Although many of these roads are the same ones we've been down before, they are different. We are different. We may pass someone along the way who looks familiar, only to realize that it was, is, or will be us in an earlier, current, or imagined

*incarnation. Like Albert Finney and Audrey Hepburn in
"Two for the Road."*

    *Joan Didion, a Central Valley refugee, once wrote
that "a place belongs forever to whoever claims it
hardest, remembers it most obsessively, wrenches it
from itself, shapes it, renders it, loves it so radically
that he remakes it in his own image." I believe that,*
Jessica admits to herself. *Modesto belongs to me and the
Central Valley is mine. I am a Central Valley Patriot. I
am a Flatlander.*

    Continuing through Graceada Park on her way
home, she is reminded of the ever-present past. The
jukebox in her head changes. The Beatles are replaced
by Joni Mitchell.

*And the seasons they go 'round and 'round
And the painted ponies go up and down
We're captive on the carousel of time
We can't return, we can only look behind
From where we came
And go round and 'round and 'round
In the circle game
And go 'round and 'round and 'round in the circle game.*

Jessica walks around inside the Bedford Falls Shop. She
gazes at the empty display case. She hears something
behind her. Startled, she spins around.

    Near the front display window and haloed by the

moonlight are her father, her mother, Johnny, Allen, and Chris.

"I haven't lost my senses," she says to them. "I've finally come to them. I'm not who I was. I've been trying so hard to bring Christmas to life, I'd forgotten that the first gift of Christmas is love. The love of a mother. Of friends. Of a community. Of a family."

She steps closer to the beloved faces.

"Your spirits. The spirits of compassion, charity, hope, forgiveness, and generosity have helped me understand that. They shall live within me all year long. Thanks to you, I now know I can learn from yesterday, live for today, and hope for tomorrow. From this day on, I will bring life to Christmas."

On her last words, the five apparitions disappear.

Chapter 25

The sun rises on Christmas morning. Jessica holds the Advent Calendar. All the days have been opened.

She pours a fresh glass of eggnog.

She sweeps up the fallen pine needles.

She winds up the musical matchbox.

She lights the peppermint candle.

She turns on the color wheel.

She puts up the decorations she had put away.

She switches on the rest of her Christmas lights inside and out.

She pops an audiocassette of Bing Crosby's *Merry Christmas* album into the cassette player. He sings "White Christmas."

Later that morning, the living room is a shambles. Wrapping paper is scattered everywhere, along with bows and ribbon, empty food plates and drinking glasses. The extended family is sprawled around the room.

All but one.

Jessica hangs the silver bell ornament on the tree. It tinkles.

"Don't you want to put it someplace safe?" Josh asks.

"This is where it belongs," Jessica answers.

The back door to the kitchen opens and closes.

"Now, who could that be?" Melissa wonders.

"It's Christmas, for Christmas sake," Dan, Jr. adds.

Just then, two boys dash into the living room followed by Michael, leaning on crutches. And Rachael.

Jessica smiles, jumps to her feet, and rushes to her brother. Beneath his pleasingly rumpled overcoat, he wears the embroidered Nutcracker pullover.

"Careful," he warns. "Don't knock me over. I'm still figuring these things out."

Jessica kisses Michael on the cheek.

"This is Rachael," he says.

"Wonderful to finally meet you," Jessica responds.

"You, too," Rachael says.

Jessica hugs Rachael.

She then corrals her two nephews, fourteen-year-old Taylor and ten-year-old Ethan, and plants an unwelcome kiss on their foreheads.

"My ex– made an exception this year. In keeping with the situation," Michael explains.

"Well, now they won't have to wait for their gifts."

Jessica takes them by the hand and leads them to a pile of presents under the tree.

Michael and Rachael follow.

The rest of the family stand.

"Rachael, meet the family. Family meet Rachael."

Michael and Rachael are quickly surrounded and smothered in affection.

As she did once before, which feels like such a long, long time ago, Jessica gazes out the set of corner windows in her kitchen. Her two faces are reflected in the windows. Janus redux.

She touches the reflection on the right – the future.

In the living room that night, everyone is pleasantly exhausted. They try on the new clothes they were given, fiddle with the new gadgets, play with the new toys.

"Can we do this again next year, Aunt Jess?" Taylor asks.

"If the fates allow," she replies.

"Awesome!" Ethan adds.

In the far corner of the room, a shimmering tableau appears.

It is Mrs. Claus, the Limping Boy, the Homeless Girl, Dudley, and George Bailey. They smile and wave, then disappear.

"It really is the most wonderful time of the year," Jessica says quietly to herself.

She finds her guitar leaning in the corner.
"This is a new one," she announces to her family. "It's called 'Counting on Christmas'."

She sings her newest song.

The smiling faces of her family fill the room with peace, love, and happiness.

In the end, Christmas wasn't the only thing I could count on to make me happy. It was family. The one thing we take for granted when it's the one thing we should treasure most.

At the end of the song, the tiny bell ornament on the tree swings to and fro with a silvery tinkle.

Jessica goes to find out what caused it to ring.

She peers closely at the ornament.

Reflected in its lustrous surface, she sees a sad woman about her own age standing on the bridge above Dry Creek, staring into the water.

Outside on the walkway leading to the house, all the *luminarias* are upright and burning brightly. The colorful Christmas lights fringing the house glow merrily. Through the large picture window stenciled with frosty Christmas images, the Christmas tree sparkles amid the joyous chaos. It resembles the last scene in the movie, *Holiday Inn*.

Jessica rejoins the circle of family and friends.

The courthouse clock chimes the midnight hour.

A full winter's moon hangs high in the night sky.

A ring circles the bright moon.

It begins to rain.

About the Author

Ken White retired from the worlds of advertising, corporate communications, and interactive entertainment to concentrate on writing and community service.

He received his A.A. degree at Modesto Junior College, his B.A. and teaching credential at UC Davis, and his M.A. at San Francisco State University. He has taught mass communications and film appreciation at Modesto Junior College.

Born in Lathrop and raised in Modesto, California, he continues to live in his hometown. He is married to Robin and has two adult step-sons, Tyler and Eric. He has written novels, screenplays, short stories, stage plays, children's and non-fiction books. Most of his stories are about his hometown and the Central Valley heartland.

https://www.facebook.com/ken.white.7106

Other Books by Ken White

Tyranny of the Downbeat
Sarah's Game
Getaway Day
Nights on the Point
That Happiness Thing: A Hometown Fable
Twelve Days of Central Valley Christmas
Touchstones: Life and Times of Modesto
Brighter Day
The Flatland Chronicles
'Twas the Night Before Christmas ... In Modesto